TRAINING DAYS

BASKETBALL IS LIFE

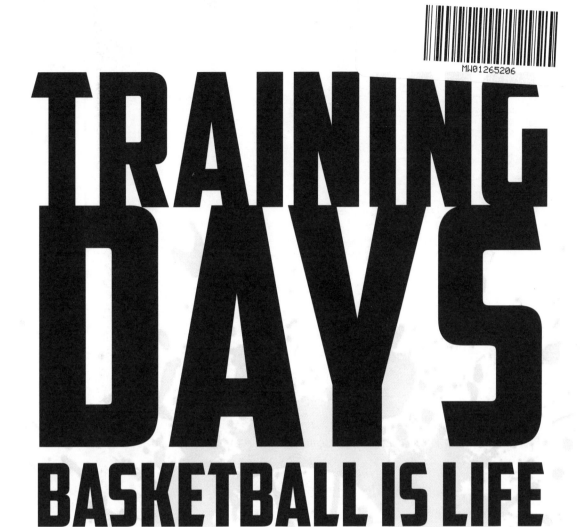

THE GROWTH NETWORK

CHRISTOPHER C. THOMPSON

Published by: The Growth Network
"We help people grow!"
www.thegrowthnetwork.org

Written by: Christopher C. Thompson
Cover Design, Interior Layout & Illustrations: Ornan Anthony, OA.Blueprints, LLC
Edited by: Tracy Thompson
Associate Editor: Tanisha Greenidge
Photography: Stephanie Hunt (Hunt2Capture)
Production Assistant: Java Mattison

Printed in the United States of America.

ISBN Paperback: 978-0-9960996-2-2

FULL-COURT PRESS

IN LOVING MEMORY OF MY DAD

CHARLES T. CHARLTON JR.
1962-2011

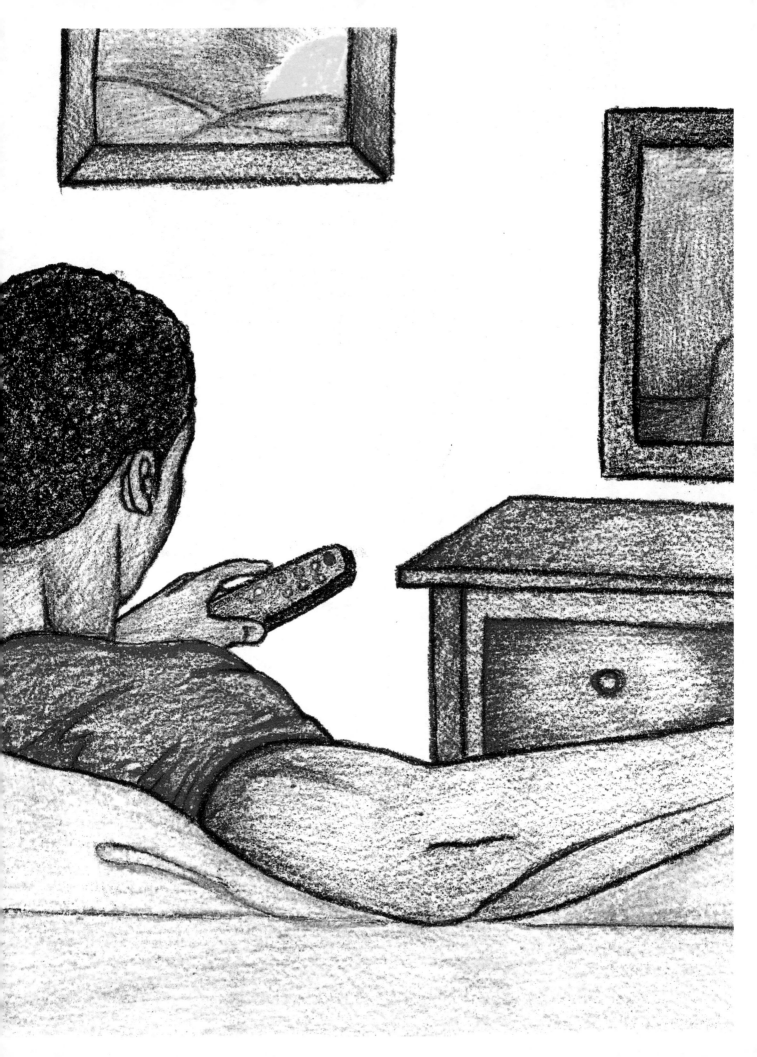

ACKNOWLEDGEMENTS

Special thank yous:
Brandon Smith, Karen Williams, Tim Lee of UMI, Christian Williams, Patty Hall, all my Beaufort peeps who keep asking, "When's the next book coming out?" To my lil sis Ashly: Where have you been all my life? To my entire Charlton fam: We're still here!

Very special thank yous:
To Tanisha, you're a beast!!! We should do all-nighters more often. To Justin, thanks for all the ideas. You're so sharp! Thanks for helping me write this...Now you may read it! Jeremy, and the entire Spirit Reign family, thanks for taking this journey with me. Tracy and Christopher you bring joy to my life and you give me limitless energy and encouragement. You two are the best part! 143!

This type of "stuff" happens every day...

THE TIP-OFF

**"All hard work brings a profit,
but mere talk leads only to poverty."**

So this is the deal. I'm still hangin' around campus because I wanted to spend the first few weeks of the summer workin' on my handles with Coach Keith and doing some strength training. Today I figured that I'd go to the records office and see if I can pick up my report card. I stop by the dorm to pick up my girl Janelle; her flight leaves today, so I wanna spend some time with her before she heads back to Atlanta. We're just gonna kick it for a minute and probably get something to eat. She's all happy to see me (like she always is).

"Well hello Mr. Sophomore!"

"Well hello Mrs. Sophomore!"

She's all amped, "I can't believe the year went by so fast...thank God we're not freshmen anymore!"

She's always high energy like that, but that's cool. That's what I like about her. She's fun, but she's smart, and she's a good, clean girl. She's not like them chicks from back home. She comes from good people.

We walk through campus, talkin' 'bout our summer plans and she's threatenin' me and sayin' that I better call her everyday, you know, the usual. So we finally get to the records office and the records lady, Ms. Lathon gives me the paper. You know the kind...the same type of envelope that they send you from the bank. You know how you gotta tear off the sides first and then tear off the top. As I take the paper from her, I just stand there staring at it. I'm scared as all get-out.

Janelle's like, "Open it! Open it!"

So I rip off the edges and fold the paper back, and I'm lookin', lookin', I read aloud to myself *Freshman Comp, Life Science, Public Speaking...* and then I stopped. I couldn't believe my eyes, "Are you serious? Are you serious? Are you serious?" My voice grows louder and louder.

Janelle's tryin' to snatch the paper from me.

She's like, "What?! What you get?!"

She snatches the paper from me and she goes nuts. She's huggin' on me, dancing, and screamin' all in the records office.

She's like, "Baby?! 4 As and 3 Bs?! That's the Dean's List AJ!"

"Yeah I know," I say to her quietly.

I could barely think. I just went outside and sat on the bench in a daze. My brain barely registers the fact that Janelle is beside me wavin' the paper and celebratin'.

"My baby got the Dean's List! My baby got the Dean's List!"

All I could think about was how much I had changed, and all the stuff that's happened to me in the past two years. Wow! It's amazing how much can change in just a couple summers. Wait till dad hears the news. I already know what he's gonna say, "Good job son. Just goes to show, there's profit in all hard work." It's funny how dad is so predictable. I'll never forget the price I had to pay to get to this point. It all started that first day of summer before my senior year in high school. Dad came home early and caught me and Shayna. That's when I learned to always make sure that the report card is addressed to me.

BY CHRISTOPHER C. THOMPSON

1

THE SCENT OF A WOMAN

"She gives no thought to the way of life;
her paths wander aimlessly, but she does not know it."

It was the last day of school so me, Chase, Clint, and Mitch de-cided to skip and play ball off campus. There's an army base real close to school and Clint's dad is military, so we all rode with Clint so he could get us through the guard check point with no problem. There's always good pick-up games on base. I guess those sol-diers have random work schedules so they workout whenever they can. The thing about playing with them army cats is that, there are hardly ever any real hoopers in the mix. Instead, what you do find are a bunch of muscle-bound G.I. Joes who foul a whole lot. But I never complain because all those guys are in good shape, and they make us work for our shots.

When we walked in the gym, some of the regulars tried to loud us out.

"Shouldn't you young bruthas be in school?" asked one of the older guys.

My boy Chase had a quick response, "Today is the last day and you don't have to go unless you had to make up a day, or make up some work." He's always the first one to come up with a lie.

We chilled and shot around for a little bit until more people came. That particular day though, there was this dude there that I had never seen before. I knew he was a baller when he walked in carrying a large black duffel bag. He was real quiet and had that swag that said he was all about business. I can always pick a true baller out of a crowd by the way he walks. And man, was I right. This dude was a beast!

I knew I wanted to "D" him up because I could tell he was good. I don't think he missed a shot during the entire game. I swear he was shooting NBA range threes and buryin' them...all net. I couldn't stop him. Not only was he pulling up from super deep, but if you tried to play him tight and take away the "J", he would blow right past you. He was super fast. His first step was ridiculous, and he had like four dunks. It was crazy!

I was kinda embarrassed, but I still talked to him after we finished playing. He said he played for a small D-1 college out in Cali, and then he played overseas for like eight years. He was nursing a knee injury and was in the states workin' out with his brother who lived on base. He gave me his information. I was thinkin' to myself like, "I'm definitely gonna hit him up."

At the time, I was talkin' to this girl named Shayna. After we left the gym, she texted me and asked me if she could come over. I knew Dad wouldn't be home for another few hours so cool, right?... Wrong!

Apparently, Dad got a call from the school principal. She told him that I might not be able to graduate if I don't get my act together. I guess he must've been havin' a bad day already, and it was a Friday, so he just cut out of work early. When he got home, he caught me and Shayna in the act in my room. It was kinda funny because she's all tryin' to fix her clothes and rush out, but he's like, "No, please don't leave on my account. Please, have a sit down." He motions us to the kitchen table.

He poured her some orange juice and starts askin' her name, and all these crazy questions like where she lives, who's her people, does she have any kids, how long has she known me and how much she really likes me. That's how I found out about the prinicpal's phone call.

"So what are your plans for after graduation?" he asked.

Shayna's not dumb. She's always sayin' she wants to be a nurse, so I know she's cool on that question. But then he keeps going.

"Would you be willing to wait for him if he doesn't graduate? Because you know he may not graduate right? See, I know you can't get admitted to college if you don't graduate, but I wonder if it's possible to play pro basketball without a high school diploma."

And now I know he's mad because he's looking right at me.

Shayna peeps the whole thing so she says, "Thanks a lot for the juice Mr. Morrow. I'm supposed to be picking up my sister from aftercare, so I gotta go."

"Okay sweetheart. You be sure to tell your mother I said hello, and that I would really like to meet her."

Dad's so old school. Who still does that? When he turns back to me, he's just grillin' me for a hot second without sayin' anything.

"Anthony, I'm really disappointed in you, but I really don't want to talk about that phone call I got today...not right now. I need some time to think about how we're going to deal with that."

I start to get up and think to myself, Whoa! I hope he doesn't try and take me off the team 'cause that's not even gonna happen. He motions me to sit back down, and then he breaks out the Bible, opens it up and starts reading:

My son, pay attention to my wisdom,
turn your ear to my words of insight,
that you may maintain discretion
and your lips may preserve knowledge.
For the lips of the adulterous woman drip honey,
and her speech is smoother than oil;
but in the end she is bitter as gall,
sharp as a double-edged sword.
Her feet go down to death;
her steps lead straight to the grave.
She gives no thought to the way of life;
her paths wander aimlessly, but she does not know it.

I was not at all prepared for what he was gonna say next.

"When I was driving home today I almost got into another accident. What's really strange is that I was thinking about your mother when it all happened. I was making a right turn and didn't even see the car coming on my left. The guy had to swerve into the other lane to avoid hitting me...I guess that's what happens when you have a lot on your mind...Did I ever tell you the story of how I met your mother? I had just broken up with this young lady that I dated pretty much all through college. I had just graduated and was working with this youth group at the church. The pastor came to the leaders and asked if we would take a small group of the seniors to a big college tour event at my alma mater. Turns out that your mother was a chaperone at that same event. We knew each other in college, but we never talked or dated. We were the youngest chaperones there, so we just walked and talked together all weekend. I knew she was interested and I was interested in her too, but I didn't want to rush into a relationship, because I had girl trouble already. But she was different. She was very sweet, funny, very intelligent, extremely winsome, and charismatic. Your mother would brighten a room wherever she went. So we became friends. I would actually ask her for advice on how I should deal with these other girls I was dating. She would laugh at me, and give me advice. Little did I know that she would be my wife just a couple years later…. A.J., let me ask you a question. On a scale of one to ten, one being worthless, and ten being priceless, how good of a woman was your mom?"

"What you mean Dad?! Mom's a twelve!"

"Okay. So now, the young lady that just left here—Shayna. That's her name right? Shayna? If you rated her on a scale of one to ten, where would she fall?"

"Uhhh…Shayna?" I stuttered. "She ain't bad, but she ain't Mom either."

"How would you rate her son?"

"I don't know Dad…five?"

"So you're telling me that you don't mind spending the rest of your life with a five when you were raised by a twelve?"

"Who said I plan on spending the rest of my life with her?"

BY CHRISTOPHER C. THOMPSON

"Son, once it is in your nose or in your clothes, it is nearly impossible to wipe or wash away the scent of a woman."

Then he just closed the Bible, got up and started fixin' dinner. We ate almost in silence. And then it was quiet for the rest of the night. I was thinkin' about what he said, but I had no idea what he meant. I thought about Shayna too. Man she's fly! I remember the first day I saw that girl. Her mom is a manager at this restaurant downtown. I thought she was older, because of what she had on, but she had so much swag and vibe that I had to say hello. That's when I found out that she was wearing the business outfit because of something she had to do at school that day. I realized that I really don't even like her all that much, but she's got the sexiest vibe about her. Her swag is intoxicating. Wait a minute...come to think of it...I guess that's his point.

At church the next day I see my boy Chase and I'm tellin' him what happened. He just shakes his head and laughs at me.

"Yo bro, your old man is madd crazy. You don't ever know what he's thinkin' cuz he be so quiet and be speakin' soft and quiet to you like he a serial killer or somethin'."

"Yeah I know. But what's crazy is that this time he didn't even say anything about the grades. He just gave me this lecture about women and not bein' able to get rid of their scent, and then when it came to the grades, he's like, 'We'll talk about it later.'"

"You think he's gonna let you go to basketball camp?"

"I dunno bro...I dunno."

So when we get home from church that day, I checked the mail, and there's my report card. So yeah, I already know what you're thinkin'. Mail doesn't run on Sunday. I know, but we go to church on Saturday...I'll explain that later.

So anyway, Dad is like, "Should I open this now and get a special Sabbath blessing or is it going to ruin my Sabbath?"

I didn't say a thing. He stood there for a while lookin' at me, and then he just dropped the paper down on the counter and walked away.

BY CHRISTOPHER C. THOMPSON

PAY NOW; PLAY LATER. PLAY NOW; PAY LATER.

"A little sleep, a little slumber, a little folding of the hands to rest—and poverty will come on you like a thief and scarcity like an armed man."

The next day, Dad says "Good mornin'" and just stays in his room for most of the day, and I just stayed in mine. I figured he was thinkin' about mom. When he told me Friday that he almost got in an accident on his way home, I knew I was in for it. Ever since mom died, dad's been sad a whole lot. He's always quiet and stuff. I think he still blames himself. So this whole thing just makes everything else so much worse.

Finally, I just got up and left the house. I figured I might as well go play some ball instead of sittin' there waitin' for the verdict. I don't even think he heard me leave. I snuck out, and ran as fast as I could to the court. When I got there, Chase was already there.

"Bro! Why you didn't call me?" I asked him.

"Bro, I figured your dad had the clamps on you."

"Man, I just bounced. I couldn't take it."

"So what he gon' do?"

"I don't even know, and I ain't even tryin' to think about that right now. I'm tryin' to play ball."

We played like three games of one-on-one. Then a few more guys came and we played a few games of thirty-three. Then we had enough people to run full, so we ran like five or six games straight. We were out there until it was dark. It was fun, but I knew I still had to go home.

It was late by the time I got back. Dad was sittin' at the kitchen table waitin' on me. Then he told me to sit down. I'm rollin' my eyes and thinkin' to myself, oh boy here we go. But deep down, I was kinda scared because I had no idea what he was about to say.

He was real calm, but he came hard from the door, "Anthony, I'm sick and tired of your disrespect, underachievement, and defiance of authority. You are on the verge of spending an extra year in high school because you aren't taking your academic responsibilities seriously. For some reason you have this idea that the rules don't apply to you because you're Mr. Basketball all over the news."

He's goin' on and on, but I was blasted when he called me Anthony. I can tell he's really mad when calls me Anthony. I tune back in, and he's still goin' off.

"Don't you know that if you want to play professionally that you're going to have put your best foot forward? You have to be coachable. You have to show a strong work ethic, commitment, and dedication in order to perform at the highest level. But all of that starts in the classroom. If you're not doing it in the classroom, how can you do it on the court? You don't even know the extent of your potential because you have yet to access it. How can you pay full attention to the playbook and game tape if you're not paying attention to your homework assignments?"

I was thinkin' to myself like, "Man, Dad's really heated." I wasn't really listenin' at first, but then I have to admit he was making a good point 'cause, I really don't be payin' attention in those team meetings.

"I've given a lot of thought to these issues son: your grades, your work ethic, your promiscuity, your attitude. I've given it all a lot of thought, and I've decided that this summer is going to be a very different summer for you. You are not gonna be free to just roam, hang around, and play basketball with your friends."

Promiscuity?! Wow! I can't remember the last time I even heard that word. I don't even wanna hear this. I wanted to jump in and say somethin' so bad, but I'm just gonna listen 'cause I don't think he's ever been this mad before.

"You are going to learn how to work this summer, and you're going to learn how to work hard. I have already talked to Brian and he needs some new people to help with the summer workload. You're going to work full-time for him at less than minimum wage. I'm not going to tell you that you can't go to your basketball camps. That's for your boss to decide whether or not he'll give you the time off. So don't stay up too late tonight because you start at 7:30 tomorrow morning."

Wow! Dad's never made me get a job. He always told me my job is to focus on my schoolwork. This is crazy! But I can't even get a word in 'cause he's not finished.

BY CHRISTOPHER C. THOMPSON

"On top of that, take this notebook and get well acquainted with it because it will be your constant companion this summer. You will use it to produce for me at least one essay each day based on a passage from the book of Proverbs. This is how it's going to work. You're going to read any passage from proverbs—it could be a verse, or an entire chapter, but you'll read it and then write your thoughts about it and how and why you think it applies to you. Don't try to cheat your way through this A.J. Read, think and write. If you try to give me three lines of nonsense, I'll have you writing essays for me until your children graduate from high school. I want at least one page for each passage, and you will do one for every day of the summer."

At this point I kinda lost it, "What if I don't?!" I blurted out.

He wasn't even fazed though. "If you don't, then I will help you find a new place to live because you will no longer be permitted to live here. I'll call your grandparents and ask them if they would allow you to live with them. Maybe you can call your Aunt Sheila and see if you can live with her and your good friend Chase. But you won't be able to stay here son. This type of defiance that you are displaying right now has to stop, or you're going to end up in a very bad place. And if you do, it won't be because I didn't try to teach you better; it will be because you refused to learn."

That's when I knew that I should just let it go because he had clearly thought this thing out. I think he knew I was gonna act like I wasn't gonna do it. He was ready for me. He had all his bases covered, and he wasn't gonna budge.

Then he just got real quiet and after a while he was like, "Do you have anything else you want to share?"

I was burnin' hot, but I said "No."

Then he just looked at me for a minute and then he went over to the fridge and started fixin' dinner. We were eatin', and it was all quiet again; just like Friday night.

After he finished eating he was like, "Be sure to clean the kitchen thoroughly."

Then he went to his room.

I just sat there for a while. I didn't even wanna finish my food. I don't know what I was thinkin' about. I was just thinkin'. After I finished cleaning the kitchen, I went to my room. I just laid down on my bed to kinda chill. That's when I started thinkin' about workin' for Uncle Brian. I guess that's not gonna be that bad. I've known Uncle Brian my whole life and he's always been cool wit' me. Well actually, he's not my blood uncle. His name is Brian Watson and he and my dad grew up together. They're like brothers, so he's like my uncle. He always helps young dudes out by givin' them jobs and stuff. Like when they get outta prison, he'll be quick to give them a job. He used to always tell Dad, "Somebody's got to give them young brothas a chance to become respectable young men and model citizens." He's always talking about how young black men need to "stop making excuses, use their heads, work hard, and start their own business." He's a cool dude. I hope he don't try to work me like a African slave. I don't even have no work boots. I ain't about to mess up my brand new Timb's on no construction site.

The next morning, Dad's callin' me, but I can't find anything that I want to get dirty. Finally, I grab some jeans that I don't wear anymore and some old basketball shoes and run out the door. As soon as I got to the site, Uncle Brian had me workin' like I was his personal house slave. They're building this house and he was sending me up and down the steps like, "Go get that wood. Go get that box of nails. Go get that cross-cut saw." Go get this. Go get that. By the time we stopped for lunch, my legs felt just like that time Coach

Keith made us run all practice long because we weren't getting back on "D" the night before. By 3:00 p.m. I was ready to quit. I was lookin' at my watch like every 15 minutes wishin' the time would go by faster. I was seriously prayin' for 5:00 p.m. to come.

When I finally got home, I was done! The only reason I didn't go jump straight in my bed is because I was madd dirty and stinkin'. I got in the shower and just stood there under the water for like twenty minutes. I was so tired I didn't even feel like grabbin' the soap. When I got out the shower I wasn't tryin' to go anywhere and it was only like 6 o'clock. Chase sent me a text sayin' that him, Mitch, Clint and Ryan were going to the city courts to play ball and they needed me to come through. We always roll like that 'cause we don't like pickin' up those whack dudes who be at the court. We like runnin' wit' our own squad. I was like, "Nah bro...I just got off work and I'm busted." That's when I realized that I hadn't even had a chance to tell Chase what had happened wit' Dad. He hit me right back.

"Wut work?!?!"

"Yeah crazy right? He made me get a job wit my uncle Brian doin construction."

"Wow bro! LOL!"

"If yall see Ronnie tell Clint dunk on that bum 4 me. I'm bout 2 go 2 sleep."

"Aight bro. holla."

"Yeah."

I put on some sweats and went right to bed. I woke up feelin' like it was a new day, but I looked out the window and it's all dark outside. Then I looked at the clock, and it's only 9:17. I saw I had a missed call from Shayna, so I called her back. No answer, but I didn't leave a message. I hate leavin' messages. What am I supposed to say? "Uhh yeah, it's me...A.J." She already knows it's me. That's why we have caller-ID. I just hung up. She'll call me back. All of a sudden I'm not feelin' her all that much anymore anyway.

I'm just sittin there on my bed, and that's when I remembered that Dad said that I gotta write a paper everyday on Proverbs. I almost forgot too. I was so tired. I was knocked out. I better write something though, just in case he checks this notebook. I grab mom's Bible, open it up, and man, I have no idea where to start...Well I guess Dad made me read chapter five the other day so I'll just go to chapter six.

Here goes nothing:

> Go to the ant, thou sluggard; consider her
> ways, and be wise:
> Which having no guide, overseer, or ruler,
> Provideth her meat in the summer, and
> gathereth her food in the harvest.
> How long wilt thou sleep, O sluggard? when
> wilt thou arise out of thy sleep?
> Yet a little sleep, a little slumber, a little
> folding of the hands to sleep:
> So shall thy poverty come as one that
> travelleth, and thy want as an armed man.

JUNE 8

PROVERBS 6:6-11

I think this is talking about being lazy. The ant is a hard worker. It says that she is a female so she must be trying to gather the food for

BY CHRISTOPHER C. THOMPSON

her babies. She works hard so her family and the rest of the ants don't go hungry. It says she doesn't have a boss telling her what to do, but she still gets the job done. I guess I need to hear that because I try to get out of doing work all the time. She does her work because it's the right thing to do. And because she knows she has to provide for her babies and the rest of the ant colony.

Then it talks about sleeping. I have to be honest about this. It's the summer and I had no intention to do anything but sleep, but I see how it's talking about how lazy people will never be successful. If I never get up out of the bed and go to the gym I will never improve my jump shot, my dribbling, and my conditioning. I want to get better. I don't want to be lazy.

It's saying that lazy people won't be successful. And actually it's saying that lazy people will be poor. I'm definitely not trying to be poor. So I guess if I want to be rich I have to work hard. I already work hard on my basketball skills, but I could work harder on my school work

As soon as I finished writin' I get a text from Shayna. She's tellin' me she's over in Park View wit' Kayla and her cousins. Those girls are madd crazy. They're always so loud. They're funny though. I just can't roll with them like that. She's like, "I'll call you as soon as we leave here." It was like 10:00 p.m. Somebody must be havin' a party. It always amazes me how people in the projects be havin' parties in the middle of the week. Why in the world would somebody be havin' a party on a Monday night? They clearly don't have a job to go to tomorrow. Man, I'm not waitin' for her to leave somebody's party to call me back. Plus, I gotta get up early in the morning. She crazy. I didn't even text her back. I'm 'bout to go to bed.

Before I knew it I was knocked out. I had a dream I was tiny like an ant walkin' around tryin' to find food. Crazy right?

At 6:30 a.m. I was wide awake and mad enough to spit nails. I was just sittin there thinkin', "I can't believe I gotta get up and do this all over again. Are you serious?!?!" I can't believe that people do this for their whole lives. I'm not even tired for real, but I just don't feel like doin' this all over again. Talk about a boring life? Wow!

By the time I got to the job site Uncle Brian was already yelling. Are you serious? Does this dude even sleep? I swear I'm 'bout to go home right now. Dad must have read my thoughts 'cause he's like, "Remember son, 'Pay now; play later. Play now; pay later.'" I grabbed my bag and went to receive my death sentence. I already know Uncle Brian's gonna try and kill me today. I don't see how the slaves did it. I would've run away so many times. They would have to cut both my legs off.

3

RED-HOT SHOOTER TO BLOODSHOT RED

*"Don't just look at the wine when it is red...in the cup
...in the end it bites like a snake and stings like a puff adder."*

My Uncle J.J. is wild! Now, Uncle J.J. is not like Uncle Brian. He's my for real, blood uncle. His real name is James Richard Morrow Jr. after my granddad. That's why they call him J.J. because he's James Jr. And that's why they call me A.J. I got my middle name from him. James. Well actually I got it from my granddad James Sr., but you get the point. I never met my granddad. Dad said he died when he was a teenager. They say he was a real good man. He was into church real heavy. He used to have his own construction business. That's how Uncle Brian got his start, 'cause he used to work for my granddad. He always talks about my granddad too. He always tells me about how granddad taught him this and taught him that. He must've made some serious bread! But anyway, Uncle J.J. ain't nothing like granddad. He's madd crazy. He used to work for granddad too so he knows his stuff when it comes to construction work, but he can't ever keep a job. So, Uncle Brian gave him a job about a week ago.

He used to work for this big construction company, but then he got fired. He used to always call dad to give him a ride to work after he was already late. Sometimes he didn't even go because he was so drunk. So now he's working with Uncle Brian. Every day after work (and sometimes at lunch) he goes to the corner store across from the job-site and buys his beer and holds it in a brown paper bag. I always wonder why those guys carry their beer in a brown paper bag while they're drinking it. I hope they're not trying to hide it because everybody already knows what it is. But, that's Uncle J.J. He always goes across the street and gets his brown paper bag. It's like a tradition for him. On Fridays he gets two bags. He gets his usual small one and a big one that he carries under his arm.

Somethin' else about Uncle J.J...He's so loud. He's always loud. He be talkin loud...laughin loud. He's just plain loud. And you can just imagine that once he gets a little bit of that beer in him he gets even louder.

Here's the thing that gets me about Uncle J.J., he's a baller. Or actually, he was a baller. When I first started getting recognized for basketball my dad would tell me these stories about him and Uncle J.J. and how they used to "run the city courts." He told me that Uncle J.J. made the all-city team, all-region team and the all-state team. He was a beast! Dad said that one time they printed a story in the paper about how good he was. The paper said that he could "single-handedly control games with his red-hot jumpshot." The story caught on around town and so everybody started callin' him "J-Red," "Red," and "J.J.-Red." It's kinda crazy 'cause now the only thing that's red about him is his eyes. If you could see Uncle J.J.'s eyes they're red all...the...time. And they're not just red, but red-red, like, fire-engine red. I guess it's all that liquor.

So one day after work he comes over to me and says, "Wussup lil' neph?" He always calls me lil' neph'.

"Ask your dad to give me a ride when he comes."

I'm sittin there thinking, "You're a grown man, ask him yourself." But I try to be at least a little respectful, so I tell him, "Come on Unc', you ask him and he'll take you."

"Naw lil' neph. Your daddy be forgettin' sometimes that I'm the big brother. Just ask him for me okay. I gotta finish somethin' real quick."

Soon as he said that I got a text from Chase.

"You comin right?"

"Waitin on my dad 2 scoop me. Where u tryna play?"

"Gardens"

"Naw bro. Those dudes got guns & they always wanna fight when they lose."

"Aight then. Green street."

"Who's all comin?"

"Errbody. Clint, Mitch, and I'm still waitin on Ryan to txt me back.

"Hit me when u get close."

"Cool"

As soon as I sent the text Dad pulled up.

"How did everything go today?"

"It was cool. Uncle J.J. asked if you can give him a ride."

"Where is he?"

"He's still inside. He said he had to finish somethin'."

"How long ago was that."

"Bout five minutes ago."

"He better hurry up because I'm not going to wait for him all evening."

"Can you drop me off at the Green Street courts?"

"Where's your gear? Don't you need to go home and get your shoes?"

"I already got my stuff in my bag."

"Well don't you want to go home and get cleaned up first?"

"Why would I waste my time gettin' all fresh and clean and then go right back out and get sweaty?"

"Okay son. I'm glad I won't be defending you."

Then Uncle J.J. comes runnin' out lookin' all silly.

"Wussup lil' bro? You can give me a ride to Terry's right?"

"James, would you please hurry up and get in the car?!"

"Oh my bad. But I dunno why you sittin' here waitin'. You could be waitin' on Brian to come out or somethin' you know. I always learned that you should never just assume. You always ask and find out first. Good lookin' out lil' neph. Oh yeah, can you pull over at the corner store?"

"Now look here James, I'm not your taxi cab. You can walk across the street, and I will do you the favor of waiting until you get back."

Uncle J.J. has this funny lookin' walk. It's like he's limpin', but he's not even hurt. He looks so silly walkin' across the street. I dunno where he got that walk from, but he looks so jacked up.

That's when dad turns around to me and asks me, "Have you done your writing for today?"

"Not yet."

"You might want to take a look at the last part of the twenty-third chapter. Start with the verse that says, 'Who has woe…'"

I'm thinkin' to myself that I might as well get it done while we're in the car cause I'm not gonna feel like doin' it when I get home tonight. I ask Dad if he's got a bible and right as I'm about to turn to the page my phone starts buzzin'. It's Shayna. She trippin' 'bout how she hasn't heard from me in like two weeks. I'm tryin' to think of an excuse so I'm like, "You know I been workin' at this construction job, and by the time I get home I'm madd tired."

"Well you could at least call me. You tryna tell me somethin'? You coulda called me!"

"It ain't even like that Shayna! Why you gettin' all loud?"

"Okay. So it ain't like that. Well what you doin' right now???"

"My Dad just came to pick me up from work. We still at the job site."

"Okay. So what you doin' when you get home?"

"I'm about to go somewhere."

"Where you goin'?"

"Why you all in my business?"

"Oh so I'm all in your business now? What you got something to hide?"

"It's not even like that. Me, Chase, Clint, Mitch, and Ryan, goin' to Green Street to play ball."

"Oh so you not too tired to go play ball wit' yo sorry little friends but you too tired to send me a text?! I got you Mister Anthony James Morr…"

"Shayna! Why you gettin' all crazy? I ain't played ball in like two weeks. I been workin' hard! You actin' all brand new 'cause I ain't talk to you, but I ain't talk to nobody these past two week…"

"She banged. That girl just banged on me."

Dad's sittin' up front chuckling like I'm on Comedy Central or some-thin'.

"Why didn't you just tell her to come to the court if she wanted to see you?"

"I can't believe that girl just banged on me."

"I'm not sure what's more amusing, the fact that she was boiling

BY CHRISTOPHER C. THOMPSON

you out or the fact that you really didn't seem like you wanted to talk to her to begin with."

"Dad I don't wanna talk about Shayna. I'm tryin' to read this chapter before I get to the court."

Dad's still just crackin' up. Shayna got me so mad. For a minute I'm just sittin' there thinkin' to myself. What's wrong with that girl? Is she crazy or somethin'? She can be real soft and sweet sometimes, but then she be gettin' all crazy. All her cousins and her friends are like that too. They be all loud and crazy all the time. She's usually the quiet one, but now I see. She can get just as crazy as the rest of them chicks.

That's when Uncle J.J. comes limpin' back over to the car.

"Hey bruh. I really appreciate this man. You remember where Terry stay right?"

Dad's just staring at him.

"He's right over there on Highland Ave on the North Side."

Everybody knows that the North Side is where all the drama's at. It's madd drugs over there. Madd drunks over there. It's crazy. We never go over there at night cause they always be shootin' and people get killed on the regular in that neighborhood. But oh well. I crack open the Bible and try to get this readin' and writin' thing done before I get to the court. Plus, by the time I get home I'm not gonna be tryin' to do anything.

"Hey Dad, where did you say start again?

"Who has woe."

Then he just grillin' Uncle J.J., and staring at him real hood like. So I'm thinkin' like, whaaaat?! Why he lookin at Uncle J.J. like that? I be feelin' sorry for Uncle J.J. sometime 'cause Dad be goin' hard on him. He don't be givin' him a break at all. But anyway, I gotta get this reading done.

Who hath woe? who hath sorrow? who hath
contentions? who hath babbling? who hath
wounds without cause? who hath redness of eyes?
They that tarry long at the wine; they that go to seek mixed wine.
Look not thou upon the wine when it is red,
when it giveth his color in the cup, when it moveth itself aright.
At the last it biteth like a serpent, and stingeth like an adder.
Thine eyes shall behold strange women, and
thine heart shall utter perverse things.
Yea, thou shalt be as he that lieth down in the
midst of the sea, or as he that lieth upon the top of a mast.
They have stricken me, shalt thou say, and I
was not sick; they have beaten me, and I felt it not:
when shall I awake? I will seek it yet again.

Dad's got this madd old Bible. I look in the front and it's got Grandad's name in it. It's got all these ol' school words in it. I was strugglin' wit' all the thines, and the shalts, and the stingeths, but I get the point. Now I know exactly why Dad was grillin' Uncle J.J. He's that guy in the verses all the way. One hundred percent. Now I know what I gotta write about.

JUNE 19

PROVERBS 23:29-35

The text I read today is about Uncle J.J. It's crazy how the Bible describes him perfectly. It's like whoever wrote this knows him personally. Or like he lived way back then. The text is describing a drunk man. He has drama. He has red eyes. He has bruises all the time. Then it describes the alcohol. It says that the drink looks smooth and smells good, but when it goes down it bites like a poisonous snake. What's funny about that is that alcohol (at least some of it) tastes good in your mouth, but it really does burn when it goes down.

Then it's like it seems like it's describing a drunk on his night on the town. He ends up walking out in the middle of the ocean and laying down like his bed is out there or something. Or either sleeping on the top of a "mast." I'm not sure what a mast is, but I will guess it's something really high, or at least it's something/somewhere he's definitely not supposed to be sleeping on.

When I read this stuff I can't help but think about Uncle JJ.

Right then and there Uncle J.J. turns around and he's like, "Ain't no homework in the summertime! Whatchu writin' bout lil' neph?!"

"You."

"You ain't writin' bout me boy! Listen here. When you wanna get a good-ol' beat down by your Uncle J.J.? You know they used to call me J.J. Red? J.J. Red...'cause my jumpshot is red-hot!"

(He's makin' that little jumpshot motion with his hands and cheesin' like he just won the lottery.)

"Uncle J.J., there's probably a law against what I would do to you if we played one on one. I could probably go to jail. I'd have all kinds of charges, assault, aggravated assault, murder, attempted murder. That's how bad I would beat you."

"Listen here lil' neph, you betta ask yo daddy 'bout me. He'll tell you I used to be a bad boy."

"Uncle J.J., you always say that. And that's why I won't take it easy on you because you always talk so much trash."

"Listen lil' neph, all you gotta do is name the time and place."

"Dad's about to drop me off at the court right now. You can come, and we can get it in today."

"See now, you know I'm going to Terry's right now. We'll get it though. Imma show you."

"How did I know you would say that?"

Then I go back to writing.

Uncle J.J. is like that guy. His eyes are always red. He always has these scars and cuts on his hands and his face. He always looks real tired in the morning as if he was up all night. And then he's drinking either coffee or Gatorade in the morning. Then I heard that people drink Gatorade to get rid of a hangover.

Uncle J.J. is always talking trash about how good he used to be in basketball. I believe him though because Dad used to always tell me stories about him and how they used to play ball. What's sad is that he never did anything with his skills. The only thing I can think of is that that alcohol messed him up. That alcohol messed him up bad. It's sad. He could've been good.

We drive up to the house and it's madd people outside across the street. Uncle J.J.'s drinkin' buddy Terry obviously lives right on the same block as the drug spot. I'm not even gonna lie, the whole time I was thinkin' like, "What if somethin' jump off right now?" The thing is, most of the time all that crazy stuff be happenin' at night. Every once in a while you hear about somebody gettin' shot in broad daylight. But still, I'm in the back seat thinkin' like I'm not even tryin' to get in the front Dad; just drive off. Finally, Dad looks back at me:

43 BY CHRISTOPHER C. THOMPSON

"I'm not your personal chauffeur A.J. Come up front."

It's so funny, but I could feel myself relaxin' when we drove off. I'm turnin' around, lookin' out the back window. At the same time I'm realizing that they not even really thinkin' 'bout us. Hey, it's cool, but I'm still gonna try and stay away from that neighborhood. It's like somethin' could go down any minute.

Then I start thinkin' about Uncle J.J. again. How can he just be chillin' over there like it's all cool? Man, that alcohol is so serious. I guess it's the same with other drugs too. You could be messed up with that stuff and get killed just because you were in the wrong place at the wrong time. It's crazy.

I just put my seat back a little bit and try to take a quick nap before we get to the court 'cause I'm already tired. Then I started thinkin'. I asked Dad, "You think Uncle J.J. coulda made it to the league?"

"That's a good question son. I think he could have. He was definitely one of the best ball players I've ever seen. And when I say that, I mean on TV or in real life. And I'm not simply saying that because he's my brother. You can ask anybody in the neighborhood who knew him back then, and they will tell you about him. As a matter of fact, Terry, his drinking buddy?...They used to play on the same summer league team."

It was silence the rest of the way. I was just layin' there trying to not think about it and at least get a few minutes of a nap.

By the time Dad dropped me off at the court everybody was already there, but I stayed on one side to shoot by myself for a while. I couldn't stop thinkin' about Uncle J.J. There was a little dude there so I had him pass me the ball and I was just workin' on my "J". Then we would switch and I would let him shoot. I was workin' with this little kid, but I don't think I've ever been so focused analyzing my shot. It's like I was workin' extra hard for Uncle J.J.; thinkin' about him not reachin' his full potential. I was on fire too! After a while, I got into my rhythm, and I couldn't miss. Once we started runnin' full court, I was already hot, and I was serious. One of the games I hit like ten threes. I wasn't really tryin' to pass. I was just focusin' on my shot. I think it made me mad that Uncle J.J. wasted his skills. I'm not tryin' to waste mine.

BY CHRISTOPHER C. THOMPSON

4

TRICKS AND TRAPS

"All at once he followed her like an ox going to the slaughter, like a deer stepping into a noose."

I've been workin' with Uncle Brian for a month now and if I had to work construction for a living then I would have to be the boss. But I'm not gonna be no boss like Uncle Brian; he works harder than his workers. I'm gonna be that dude at the job site with the clean work boots tellin' everybody else what to do. I mean, what's the point of bein' the boss if you the one doin' all the work? I gotta have an easy job. Man I been workin so hard, it's Sunday, and just thinkin' 'bout work right now is makin' me tired. I don't feel like goin' to work tomorrow at all. It's crazy too 'cause yesterday was the Fourth of July and I'm thinkin' like why does the Fourth of July have to fall on a weekend? Why couldn't it be on Monday so we could have the day off? So I'm gonna get all I can outta this weekend. My crew is tryna play ball today, so Imma link up with them later, but today is a total chill day.

So now, speaking of Fourth of July, Shayna sends me a text askin' if I wanna go with her to this cookout, but I have no intention of goin' anywhere with that chick. I had a good excuse though 'cause it was the Sabbath and Dad's not even tryna hear that. So I text her back and tell her, "Dad's not havin it. We goin 2 church."

"On Saturday?"

"We go to church every Sat."

"U go to church on Saturday and Sunday?"

"Naw. Jus Sat."

"Who goes to church on Saturday?"

"Me and a whole bunch of other people"

"That's the wrong day."

"U need to read ur Bible. Sat is the right day. Sun is the wrong day."

"How u figure?"

"Read exodus 20:8-11"

What she doesn't know is that I have no desire to talk to her right now. I haven't talked to her for real ever since that day she called me getting all crazy and then banged on me. She called me that Sunday like nothing ever happened. I knew she knew I hadn't for- got about it and I was at the gym so we didn't even talk long. She's been textin' me ever since and I ain't rushin' to text her back. So I think she knows I'm not really feelin' her no more. What's crazy is, that same day she called me when I was at the gym, this girl that Chase is messin' with named Keisha walked in with two other girls.

I've never seen them before, but they're all giggling and whispering the whole time. Girls always giggling at the court.

Sometimes I wanna tell them to just "Shut up!" But anyway, Keisha is fly. She's short, brown skin, and she's got a bangin' body. The other one's name is Natasha. She aight, but she's the one with the car so she get a few points for that. Mitch said her dad's got serious bank. So she get a few extra points for that too. But the light skinned one look like a supermodel. She got a blazin' body, but her face is something off a magazine cover. I've never seen her before, but this girl is gonna be famous!!! Shorty needs her own reality show. Trust me.

But we're in the middle of a game though and I'm not trying to lose. We were up 5-3, and everybody's lookin' over at the girls. So I gave Chase the signal and we trapped their point at like half court. He could dribble a little bit, but when he saw the trap he just got shook. Easy steal. Easy basket. 6-3. Now that we know that he's shook, we trapped him again. This time he tried to give it up quick and throw it over my head. Easy steal. Easy dunk. 7-3. The next time, he gave it up real early. The game was too easy. They couldn't stop us. We ended up trappin' my dude like two more times. 8-3, 9-3. It got outta hand real fast. Game over. 16-5.

So after we finish hoopin', I ask Keisha to introduce me. So she's like, "This is my friend Jade. Jade this is A.J." Shorty walks over and she's got jokes already, but she's real smooth and sweet wit' it. "She's like, "I know you, you go to my school. And you're always on the news and in the paper, but I've seen you play and I figure they must not have anyone or anything else to talk about at all." I swear she's lyin' because I would know if there was somebody this fine at my school. But I go along wit' it though.

"Oh so you're a comedian?"

"Naw, I'm more like a news anchor. I just tell it like it is."

She's got this beautiful smile. Perfect teeth. She must use those whitening strips or somethin'. Keisha's walkin' away like, "Imma let ya'll talk, I gotta go pee." Keisha's so ghetto. Why she gotta share all that information? Anyway, I've never met a girl who I thought was perfect, but this chick is like the spokeswoman for Dime-piece International. Everybody was leavin' the gym so we just chilled and talked outside. Chase jumps in the car wit' Keisha and Natasha. I could tell she was feelin' me 'cause her girl Natasha was yellin' at her tryna rush her but she was like, "Go 'head. I'm just gonna walk. I'll call y'all later." Apparently she lives in the projects right by the gym. We were out there for like two hours, just talkin'. She's madd sweet, super cool. Got a really good sense of humor. She's not all ghetto and crazy. She into weird stuff like country music and horses and stuff, but she listens to rap too. It's kinda weird, but it shows she's different. She's not like every other girl. So I walked her home and then I walked home.

I thought about her the whole way home. I'm tryin' to call Chase and ask him why he never introduced me to her before, but he's not answering. He must've went to Keisha's house. So I just shot him a text. She texted me as soon as I walked in the door.

"U home yet?"

"So wut u my mother now?"

"Naw I just don't want nothing 2 happen 2 you before u actually learn how 2 play ball. U seem 2 work so hard at it."

"lol. Here you go wit da jokes."

"I told u I just tell it like it is."

We pretty much stayed on the text piece all night, back and forth till I fell asleep. Real talk, shorty's wifey material.

So I wake up, time to get ready for work and Jade is on my mind heavy. I'm trippin' for real, but I'm not tryna text her right now 'cause I don't wanna seem like I'm stalkin' her. So I just try to switch my mind to something else, and that's when I realize I forgot to write yesterday. So I just figured I'd ask Dad if I could skip that day.

"Dad, I forgot to write in my notebook."

"Well Son, what are you planning to do about it?"

"Well, I was hoping that since I haven't missed any days, I could just skip that day."

"Was that our agreement?"

"No."

"Okay, I'll tell you what, since you seem to be taking this pretty seriously, this is what we can do. I haven't looked at your notebook yet but I'm going to read it tonight. And when I look at it today's entry needs to be exceptional. I mean exceptional. No half baked ideas. I want you to really think about what you're reading and respond with your writing. How does that sound?"

"I can do that."

As soon as we pulled up to the job site I just knew it was gonna be a hard day. I got out the car and Uncle Brian is already yellin' at the crew. Apparently, somebody jacked up something the day before and now we gotta fix it. Hey, I know it's not my fault because I'm just like the little errand boy. I don't do no cutting, no measuring; none of that stuff. I do a little bit of hammerin', but that's as deep as it gets. But still, it was a rough morning 'cause Uncle Brian was stressin' hard. So everybody was workin' extra hard, no laughin', no jokin'. All you could hear was the oldies station playin' on Uncle Brian's yellow radio.

As soon as lunch time came I found myself a corner to just chill. We barely even took a water break since we started this morning. That's when I saw that I missed a text from Chase.

" What happened wit Jade"

He sent it like an hour ago, but I figure I'd hit him right back. He'll get it.

"She's tight bro. How come u never told me about her?"

"I thought u already knew her."

"Wut? I never seen that girl b4 in my life."

"So wut happened?"

"She's cool bro. We jus chilled talked."

"Wut u mean u just chilled n talked?"

"Wut u in the slow class now? We jus talked. U don't talk to girls no more?"

"Bro u coulda hit that so easily. Errbody n they lil brotha done hit that. Dudes b callin her Jaws cuz she give crazy head. n I heard she do girls 2"

"R u serious bro?"

"I wudnt lie bout sumthin like this madude. That's y I axed u if u hit? I cudnt answer u back cuz I went 2 Keisha's n hit. Her mom n vegas so I spent the nite. Txt Jade n c wut she doin 2nite ."

I'm just sittin' there in a daze kinda 'cause I couldn't believe what Chase just told me. How could a girl that fine be that grimy? I remember hearin' them dudes jokin' bout a girl named Jaws, but I had no idea who they were talkin' 'bout so I just let it ride. So right then Uncle Brian starts yellin' 'bout how lunch is supposed to be over. I went back to work and I had already been thinkin' about her, but now I couldn't stop thinkin' about the fact that she is actually a trick. I kept asking myself, "How could a woman so beautiful, be so nasty?" That stuff is crazy. And yo, I'm not tryin' to roll like the last cart on the train. I ain't never liked leftovers. But what's even more crazy is that this girl is so tight beyond just the looks. She got a tight personality, she not just loud and ghetto, she's interested in different stuff. But man!!! She damaged goods. I just can't do it. That joint had me messed up for the rest of the day.

So as soon as I get off, how 'bout I got like three texts from Jade. And man, really? I'm not even tryin' to respond. Real talk, I'm actually a little sad 'cause I thought she was special, but she worst than a lot of these girls out here in the hood. I can't get down. Normally, I might have even thought about just hittin' it and then cuttin' her off, but ever since Dad was talkin' to me about Mom and rating girls compared to her, I been lookin' at girls in a whole different way. So now I'm tryin' to think of a smooth way to blow her off.

Uncle Brian gave me a ride home 'cause dad said he had to work late. As soon as we pull up to the house Chase and Mitch are waitin' for me outside. He sent me a text to say he was comin' over but I didn't know he was tryna meet me there.

"Yo, so wussup wit' Jade? We was gonna go link up wit her, Keisha, and Tasha."

"Yo bro, ya'll can go ahead. I'm not messin' wit' dat chick."

"Dude what you mean? Dat's like sayin' I don't want a free Big Mac from McDonalds."

"First of all I don't even like McDonalds. Second of all, in all the years that you known me, when have I ever even been seen wit' a bad news chick?"

"I gotta give you that. I never seen you wit' no lame broad."

So at first Mitch is just listenin' with this confused look on his face, but then he just jumps right in with that same confused look and a question.

"So you tellin' me that if that chick was naked right now wit' you and throwin' it at you, you wouldn't hit?

All of a sudden everybody is silent. It's like we all had the picture in our minds or something. We just sat there starin' for a minute.

"See! That's what I thought."

"Naw, hold on…Real talk?…Nope!"

"Aaaahhhhh!!!! Here he go!!! AJ you's a lame."

"Dude you never know this chick could have AIDS or something. And seriously, I'm not tryna mess wit' no more girls from round here. All these girls are madd grimy, and loud, and ghetto.

Then Mitch jumps back in. He seems to be too overwhelmed wit' the idea of me not feelin' Jade.

"Are we talkin' 'bout the same Jade?!?! Shortie is fire!"

"Exactly and I'm not tryna get burned. But that's not the point. "

"So what is the point?"

"I'm just sayin' it's not all about looks."

"You right cause even if shortie need a brown paper bag, and she throwin' it at me, Imma knock it out the park."

"Man, you better catch it and throw it back."

"You slippin' A.J. You slippin'."

That's when Dad pulled up. He gets out the car and everybody gets quiet. He's just staring at us and then he's like, "What's wrong fellas, cat got your tongue? Mitchell, Andre, what's up guys?"

"Sup Mr. Morrow?"

"Sup?"

"What are you guys getting into?"

"Just chillin' dad."

"No basketball today?"

"Not for me. I'm so busted! Uncle Brian tried to kill us today. I couldn't shoot one jumper if I tried."

"A.J. do you have something for me yet?"

"Not yet Dad, I just got home."

"Okay, son. I'm looking forward to it."

Dad heads up the steps and everybody just standin' there quiet like we're all ready to just break out. Chase is messin' with his cell phone, and Mitch is scraping something off the bottom of his Air Forces. I broke the silence first.

"Aight yall, I'm 'bout to go in here and write this paper."

"Paper? Nigga you in summer school and you workin?!"

"Naw bro. His dad got him on some straight journal writin' type joint for a punishment."

"Yo, Mr. Morrow be on dat Malcom X, Marcus Garvey, Martin Luther King!!! He always like that?"

"Always ma'dude. Always."

"Aight m'nigga we holla at you lata."

"Yeah bro."

I'm just about to walk in the door when Chase is like, "Yo is that Toya over there?"

"Yeah that's her."

"Yo, I'm 'bout to go holla."

"Weren't we just talkin' bout getting burned?...I know that joint is flammable!"

"Naw bruh. I always got a glove."

"Aight Mr. Fireproof. Just remember, fire melts plastic."

"Yes sir, Mr. Morrow sir."

Then, I guess Mitch was wantin' to get in the action so he's like, "Man, I'm 'bout to holla at Tasha." Chase is on some reckless joint 'cause he's like, "Yo! That's wussup, you hit Tasha up and tell her to bring Keisha, and as soon as I get back on that side Imma come through." The whole time, I'm just standing there lookin' at them, shakin' my head.

"Aight y'all. Be easy."

"Aight."

"Holla."

I figure I might as well get started on this paper while I still feel like doing it. When I walk in the house, I plopped down on the floor in the hallway to take my boots off. I completely ran through those sneaks I had in like the first two weeks, so I broke down and bought some cheap work boots. Dad is standing by the living room window just staring. I feel like I need a crowbar to pry my feet out of these boots. After all that going up and down those half-done stairs, all that sweatin' and workin' it feels like my feet, sock and boots are sealed together.

"I didn't know Chase was dating Latoya."

"What you talkin' bout Dad? Chase isn't datinnng anyone!"

"Are you sure?"

By now I'm wanting to see what he's talkin' about, so I walk over to the window and sure enough there's Chase and Toya all in each other's personal space.

"Was that what you all were discussing when I drove up?"

"Basically."

"Well then maybe you ought to read chapter seven."

"The whole thing."

"Well, you don't have to read the entire chapter, but reading the entire chapter will give you greater insight into what it means."

"Ok."

I sit down, crack open the Bible and I can't believe what I'm looking at.

My son, keep my words
and store up my commands within you.
Keep my commands and you will live;
guard my teachings as the apple of your eye.
Bind them on your fingers;
write them on the tablet of your heart.
Say to wisdom, "You are my sister,"
and to insight, "You are my relative."
They will keep you from the adulterous woman,
from the wayward woman with her seductive words.
At the window of my house
I looked down through the lattice.
I saw among the simple,
I noticed among the young men,
a youth who had no sense.
He was going down the street near her corner,
walking along in the direction of her house
at twilight, as the day was fading,
as the dark of night set in.

Then out came a woman to meet him,
dressed like a prostitute and with crafty intent.
(She is unruly and defiant,
her feet never stay at home;
now in the street, now in the squares,
at every corner she lurks.)
She took hold of him and kissed him
and with a brazen face she said:
"Today I fulfilled my vows,
and I have food from my fellowship offering at home.
So I came out to meet you;
I looked for you and have found you!
I have covered my bed
with colored linens from Egypt.
I have perfumed my bed
with myrrh, aloes and cinnamon.
Come, let's drink deeply of love till morning;
let's enjoy ourselves with love!
My husband is not at home;
he has gone on a long journey.
He took his purse filled with money
and will not be home till full moon."
With persuasive words she led him astray;
she seduced him with her smooth talk.
All at once he followed her
like an ox going to the slaughter,
like a deer stepping into a noose
till an arrow pierces his liver,
like a bird darting into a snare,
little knowing it will cost him his life.
Now then, my sons, listen to me;
pay attention to what I say.
Do not let your heart turn to her ways
or stray into her paths.
Many are the victims she has brought down;

her slain are a mighty throng.
Her house is a highway to the grave,
leading down to the chambers of death.

So I'm not quite sure where to start because this chapter got me thinkin' 'bout Shayna, Jade, Keisha, Tasha, Toya, and just about every other girl I've ever met in the hood. I was thinkin' about girls that I had done wrong and girls that I knew from the jump were bad news. I was thinkin' 'bout Chase sleepin' over at Keisha's while her moms was outta town. I was thinkin' 'bout Jade and how she could be so tight and so grimy at the same time. I was thinkin' 'bout all that stuff. So I know Dad said that he wanted it to be extra good but I was thinkin' about so much so fast that I didn't want to forget any of it so I just started writing whatever came to mind next.

JULY 6
PROVERBS 7

I would be lying if I said that I didn't see myself in this chapter. Honestly, I see all of my friends in here because we all do the same thing. We all go chasing after girls for one thing and one thing only. None of us are even thinking about getting married. We all want the same thing☺sex. The thing is when we get with this girl there is always a catch.

In the story, the girl is actually married and she tricks the guy into coming to sleep with her while her husband is out of town. The problem is that she has done this many times before because it says that she has many victims.

I don't know anybody personally who has caught AIDS or some other serious disease, but I know a whole bunch of people that have gotten beat up and some of them even killed over a girl. And even if you don't get beat up or killed, most of the time the girl turns out to be crazy. A lot of times the girl turns out to be possessive and jealous like she's your wife or something. She's getting all upset and cursing you out because you haven't called her when she's the one who gave it up too easy.

What's really sad is that you don't even have to have sex with the girl for her to start acting like she's your wife and you belong to her. Sometimes girls are just needy like that. Speaking of needy girls, there's also that girl who gives it up real easy and then tries to make it seem like it's your fault and that you took advantage of her. So she's trying to put you on a serious guilt trip like it's your fault that she's easy.

Then there's the other side of jealousy where the girl gets totally crazy and violent. She's cussing you, threatening you, stalking you, all because she felt like you did her wrong. I know guys who got their cars keyed, tires slashed, windshield busted, and all kind of stuff. I've even seen a guy's new girl get beat down in the street by this girl and her cousins all because he didn't want to talk to her anymore.
Then there is the whole thing with other guys who like the girl, and the girls brothers or male cousins who sometimes want to get involved. It always amazes me why dudes will fight over a girl. And sometimes dudes even get killed over girls. This dude named Dorien from the north side just got shot a couple weeks ago over a girl. What's crazy is, it was his own homeboy that shot him.

I guess I'm starting to realize that it's a big game. But it's not fun anymore. Because in the end you always end up getting caught up just like the guy in the story. It's like getting caught in one of those big bear traps like on the cartoons. Once you get your foot caught in that thing, you'll never be able to get it off. It's just not worth it.

I kept writing until it all came out and I was outta ideas. I looked back at what I had written and I couldn't believe I wrote so much.

It was kinda weird because everything I wrote was right off the top of my head and it was the first time I was writing what was really on my mind. I mean, this is the first time I wasn't just tryin' to write somethin' just to get it done. I think I'm really startin' to think more about some things.

I was just sittin' there kinda messed up thinkin' and stuff. I had a lot on my mind. Then my phone starts ringin'. It's Chase, he's laughin' all loud and breathin' so hard I could barely understand what he was sayin'.

"Yo bro, that joint was crazy!"

"Whatchu talkin' bout bro?"

"Yo bro, Toya is so wild bro! I walk over to her and it's on before I even open my mouth. She like ain't you Dre's cousin, and I'm like yeah and after that it was poppin'. So long story short she takes me straight to the crib and she's goin' hard like, 'So wassup?' Like she challengin' me or somethin'. We goin' at it from the door. We go up stairs to her room and we up for there like five minutes when her moms comes home. I have no intention of gettin' caught in this house so I dipped across the hall to the bathroom and there's a window in the bathroom. So I climb out the window. Now the roof on that side of the house is not that high, but it's high enough to where I'm not just gonna jump off. Plus I'm not tryna break no bones. Plus I don't want her moms to hear me. So I roll, I get on my stomach and I try to slide off the roof. Problem is them shingles jacked up my polo shirt. Man, and I just got this shirt too! So anyway, I slide off the roof and I ran. Shorty is wild though, and I know where she live, but I ain't even have a chance to get her number. That joint was crazy!"

I'm not sure what I was thinkin'. Everything was racing through my mind so fast. I didn't say anything though. I was just thinkin'. Dad always says that it's good to just sit and process things sometime.

"Think about it," he says. So I was thinkin'...hard.

"You there bro?"

"Naw, I mean yeah. Yeah, I'm here."

"You ain't say nothin."

"I was just workin' on this writin' my Dad got me doin'."

"I hear you. Well look bro, Imma bout to go holla at Mitch and Keisha. I'll hit you up later."

"Aight bro, be careful out there man."

"What you my dad now? Listen bro...My name is Chase, and I stay on da chase. And you can chase me if you want, but I'm winnin' da race. They never catch me. Never touch me. Never see me. And all da lil' dudes on the block, they wanna be me. "

"Okaaay, so you're like the gingerbread man rapper."

"Ahhhhh!!! Haha A.J. very funny."

"I'm just sayin bro, that's what the gingerbread man said."

"Yeah, yeah. Aight bro, I'll holla."

"Aight bro. Peace."

HIT A LICK

*"These men lie in wait for their own blood;
they ambush only themselves."*

Uncle Brian said we could stop workin' kinda early today because we're ahead of all the other contractors. He said we can't really go any further until they come in and do their parts. Uncle Brian dropped me off at home, so I called Chase to see if he wanted to go play ball.

"Yo bro, you know I'm game, cuz I got game. And don't hate cuz and try t'test cuz I'll put you to shame. Y'all know da name, it's Chase Freeman y'all. Baggin' chicks and pushin' fast breaks, blowin' by 'em, throwin' dimes when they go for my head fakes."

"Dude, why you always rappin' to me? This ain't no concert, and I'm not a fan."

"Yo bro, speakin' of concert, you goin' to the concert this weekend?"

"What concert?"

"The Get Money tour is gon' be here this weekend. J-Millz, Lil Mama, DJ Dirty Fingaz, Mr. Fantastic; it's a whole bunch of them."

"Naw bro. You know they gon' be shootin' out there."

"Man, you better learn how to duck or else you not gon' be able to go nowhere."

"Besides, I'm not tryin' to pay money to stand in some crowded place wit' a whole bunch of loud, sweaty, black people, actin' crazy. If I wanted to hear their music, I would just buy it or turn on BET or MTV."

"You should come through bro. It's gon' be tight."

When we got to the court there really wasn't anybody there so we shot around for a little while and then we started playing one on one. After a little while three guys came in from the Southside. I know those cats. They're cool wit' us, but their school team is wack. We smash them all the time. Last time we played them, I dropped thirty-two. They said, "Wussup?" but then they went straight to the other side of the court and started shootin' around by themselves. They didn't even ask could they break in the game. After a while some dudes came in that I've never seen before. They came in with their own five, so it's pretty obvious, they plan to play together and stay together. At first they were just standin' on the side talkin', but as soon our game was over one of them came over to us like, "Let's run full. Y'all five against our five."

Me and Chase are lookin' at each other like naw, because we're used to beatin' on them Southside cats; we don't ever play with them. But hey, they already got their five so it's whatever. But then I start lookin' at our squad and I'm like, "Ok. We got some pieces."

First off, Chase is the best PG I know. He's madd short but he's got enough swag for about three or four big, tall, fat dudes. Then there's Tyrell. Everybody calls him Ty. He has no handles whatsoever, but he's super fast and he's got good hands. Homie gets madd steals like the cat burglar. This other cat, Trey got the perfect name because he got a wet spot up jumper. He can't hit wit' somebody in his face, but if you leave him open it's lights out. Then there's Drew, he's chunky and he be hackin', but he grabs rebounds though. And come to think of it all that foulin' might help us a little bit because these dudes are kinda big.

So from the very beginning I could tell they were sleepin' on us. They weren't that good though. They just got this one dude; and he don't miss. Super quick first step. And he's got serious range. We kinda play alike, and he's clearly the best. So, I know I need to "D" him up. But the rest of them weren't that good. We got out ahead of them real quick. The score was like 6-2 and they were already arguing with each other. We were kinda in the zone though, so we just kept playin'. We were movin' the ball and hittin' our open shots. Ty keeps pickin' my man's pockets and we're off to the races. So one time they bring the ball up and Ty picks this guy again. He hits me on the wing and I only got one person to beat. But as soon as I get to the three point line one of their dudes comes chargin' through the lane to stop the penetration. That's when I saw Trey spot up in the corner. I dish it off to him and, BANG! We're up 8-2.

They're real mad now. On the next play their superstar gets the ball. I should say he's the one who was real mad, 'cause homie got the ball in his hands and I was definitely sure he was gonna shoot. Every scorer gets that look in their eyes when they're determined to score. I just couldn't stop it. He's one of those cats with perfect form and he jumps high whenever he shoots. So I wasn't giving him that much space but he gave me a lil' in-and-out dribble and then he pulled up from deep…bottoms!!! 8-4. Dude can shoot for real! But then Drew snatched it out the net and threw a football pass to

Chase for a quick layup. 9-4. At this point it's obvious that we're just plain faster than these dudes.

By now, the gym is getting crowded. This stuff happens all the time. It's like everybody is just lookin' for the gym where it's goin' down. People will come in and peek to see if there is anybody inside. If there's only a few people they'll leave and go somewhere else. If there's a crowd they stay. I guess they're lookin' for the spot where they're guaranteed to get some full court games in. Anyway, we were already runnin' so I guess they all decided to stay.

Meanwhile, we're giving these dudes the business. Not only are we faster than them, but they need a new PG 'cause dude brings the ball up and Ty robs him again. Chase is like, "Call the cops," and Ty takes a few dribbles and then hits him with a quick outlet pass. Chase cuts to the middle of the court and our poor little robbery victim is trying to chase him down. He has no idea that he's right behind Chase, but I'm right behind him. He never saw it coming, but Chase saw me the whole time. He jumps to block what he thought was a layup but Chase put it off the glass nice. I caught it with two hands and yammed it!!! The whole gym went crazy. All you heard was, "OOOOOOOOHHHH!!!!" Dudes were laughin', dappin' each other up. It was crazy! 10-4.

After that we kinda got sloppy and they started comin' back. Before we knew it the score was 13-11, 14-12, then 14-14. Now our team is mad 'cause they could hit a 2 pointer and win. But then Superstar missed a 2 and they left Trey wide open again when we got the ball back. 16-14. Game over! They were heated. They swore up and down that they could beat us. But, step to the sideline, put your name on the list, and wait for another chance.

We ran like three more games straight. Then those same dudes got back on and beat us 18-16. Oh well, it was a good run though. I'm madd tired so I'm goin' straight home, but when we were walkin' outside Chase's cousin Dre was walkin' in. Chase is like, "Yo, was-sup fam!?!? You hoopin'?!"

"Naw fam, I came here lookin' for you. Wuss good?"

Then he turns and sees me and he's like, "Yoooo!!! Wuss good young superstar?!?!"

"Chillin' bro."

Then he turns back to Chase and he's like, "Yo lemme holla at you for a min lil' cuz."

I already know something's not right 'cause I swear I ain't never seen Dre on nothin' positive, and I ain't never seen this cat at the gym. He's a real hood dude. He's cool, but he's street and every-body already know what it is.

"So then Chase is like, "Yo bro, Imma hit you up later."

"Aight bro!"

"Aight young superstar. Be safe."

"Aight bro."

It's kinda funny when you think about it. These street dudes always take this protector type role with the young dudes as if they're up-standing, law-abiding citizens. They always say stuff like "Stay in school." "Be safe." "Stay outta trouble." As if that's what they plan on doing. It's crazy. I guess deep down a lot of those cats ain't all bad, but they just get caught up. But it's still kinda funny hearin' them say it.

I walked home and just chilled. I got a text from Jade. I almost forgot about shortie, but hey...

"Wut u doin?"

"Just finished hoopin. Bout 2 get ready 4 work."

"How come u never get at me?"

"Work...busy"

 "A simple txt wud b nice"

"I feel u"

All of a sudden, I'm reminded why I really liked this girl. She's got serious flava. She just damaged goods. Otherwise I would really be tryna holla at her. I don't know man...maybe I can just be cool with her. Crazy stuff.

"I gotta write this thing for my dad and then I'll call u."

"K"

All this time I been reading proverbs and I don't think I ever read chapter one. I crack it open and I figure...well...it's kinda long but Imma try and read the whole thing.

The proverbs of Solomon son of David, king of Israel:
for gaining wisdom and instruction;
for understanding words of insight;
for receiving instruction in prudent behavior,
doing what is right and just and fair;
for giving prudence to those who are simple,
knowledge and discretion to the young—

let the wise listen and add to their learning,
and let the discerning get guidance—
for understanding proverbs and parables,
the sayings and riddles of the wise.
The fear of the LORD is the beginning of knowledge,
but fools despise wisdom and instruction.
Listen, my son, to your father's instruction
and do not forsake your mother's teaching.
They are a garland to grace your head
and a chain to adorn your neck.
My son, if sinful men entice you,
do not give in to them.
If they say, "Come along with us;
let's lie in wait for innocent blood,
let's ambush some harmless soul;
let's swallow them alive, like the grave,
and whole, like those who go down to the pit;
we will get all sorts of valuable things
and fill our houses with plunder;
cast lots with us;
we will all share the loot"—
my son, do not go along with them,
do not set foot on their paths;
for their feet rush into evil,
they are swift to shed blood.
How useless to spread a net
where every bird can see it!
These men lie in wait for their own blood;
they ambush only themselves!
Such are the paths of all who go after ill-gotten gain;
it takes away the life of those who get it.
Out in the open wisdom calls aloud,
she raises her voice in the public square;
on top of the wall she cries out,
at the city gate she makes her speech:

BY CHRISTOPHER C. THOMPSON

"How long will you who are simple love your simple ways?
How long will mockers delight in mockery
and fools hate knowledge?
Repent at my rebuke!
Then I will pour out my thoughts to you,
I will make known to you my teachings.
But since you refuse to listen when I call
and no one pays attention when I stretch out my hand,
since you disregard all my advice
and do not accept my rebuke,
I in turn will laugh when disaster strikes you;
I will mock when calamity overtakes you—
when calamity overtakes you like a storm,
when disaster sweeps over you like a whirlwind,
when distress and trouble overwhelm you.
"Then they will call to me but I will not answer;
they will look for me but will not find me,
since they hated knowledge
and did not choose to fear the LORD.
Since they would not accept my advice
and spurned my rebuke,
they will eat the fruit of their ways
and be filled with the fruit of their schemes.
For the waywardness of the simple will kill them,
and the complacency of fools will destroy them;
but whoever listens to me will live in safety
and be at ease, without fear of harm."

I'm really starting to feel this. I read the whole chapter and it was deep. I couldn't believe that the Bible was describing some dudes planning to rob somebody. It immediately made me think about seeing Dre earlier. I know he was on some other stuff. I just hope he wasn't tryin' to get Chase to ride wit' him.

I fell asleep and didn't even write anything. I didn't even call Jade back. The next morning I was getting ready to go to work and my Dad was watchin' the news. That's when I saw it. I just froze. The story was about a robbery and a shootout with the cops. One cop was shot and one of the suspects killed...Andre Freeman.

"Isn't that Jason's boy?"

"Dad, he was just at the court yesterday...I hope Chase wasn't there."

I called Chase, but he didn't answer. Then I texted him.

"I just saw the news bro. wut happened?!?!"

No answer.

I was quiet all morning. I was just thinkin'.

At lunch time I tried to call Chase again. No answer. So I sent him another text. "Hit me up as soon as u get dis." I couldn't even eat. I just pulled out my notebook and started writing.

I can't even describe what I'm thinking right now. My man Chase's cousin Dre got shot by the cops last night trying to rob one of them Asian corner stores. What's crazy is that, I had just seen him earlier that day when I was leaving the gym. It's crazy how you see some-body one minute, and they're laughing and smiling and the next minute they're gone, and they're never coming back.

What makes the whole thing so much worse is that I think my boy Chase was there. The news says that no arrests were made and they were still looking for the suspects, but I'm worried because he's not answering his phone.

Right then I realized, I never called Aunt Sheila. When she said hello,

BY CHRISTOPHER C. THOMPSON

I could tell that she was crying.

"Hey Aunt Sheila, this is A.J. I saw the news. I just called to see if Chase was alright."

"Ohhh A.J. Baby, I was hopin' that you had heard from him, cause I haven't seen him since yesterday mornin.'"

"I tried callin' and textin' him, but I didn't get no answer."

"I talked to his Uncle Jason and, he said Keisha said they had seen Chase and Dre together over by the PJs."

"Well I know he was with Dre because when I got off of work yesterday we went and played ball and Dre was comin' in the door when we were walkin' out. They started talkin' and I was madd tired so I just left and went home."

"Well the police came by here earlier lookin' for him so if you hear from him, please tell him to call his mother."

"Yes ma'am."

"Love you baby."

"Love you too Auntie."

"Okay, bye bye."

"Later."

Okay, so now I'm almost positive that Chase was there, and he's probably tryin' to lay low 'cause he knows the cops is gonna be out right now. So I called Mitch to ask him if he heard anything. Mitch said, "Yo bro it's crazy out here. Them boys been ridin' by here all mornin' and they just got Twiz, just now. They puttin' him in the car as we speak."

"Who is Twiz?"

"Dats Dre's homie. Them cats is like boyfriend and girlfriend. They always together."

"You seen Chase?"

"Naw bro. You?"

"Naw. This cat won't answer his phone."

"Yo, everybody sayin' he was wit' them bro."

"I know."

"Yo I can't believe that dude Dre is gone. Crazy right?"

"Super crazy. I just saw this cat at the gym yesterday."

"Word?"

"Word."

"Crazy."

"Yo I gotta go. Hit me up if you hear anything else."

"Aight bro."

"Peace."

"One."

I only had a few minutes left before lunch was over, but I wanted to finish writin' down what I was thinkin'.

It's getting really crazy in the hood. There's always something going on, somebody getting shot, shot at, robbed, or something like that.

I never thought I would be the one to admit that the Bible was right. I mean, I've always believed the Bible was true, but I never seen it be so real. It's almost like somebody was sitting down in the hood writing about what was happening right in front of him.

I pray that Chase is okay. And I pray for Dre's dad cause I know he's going through it right now.

All I know is I hope Chase is okay. Lunch time is over so I gotta get back to work. There wasn't much time to stress over the streets though 'cause after lunch Uncle Brian raised the bar like five notches. We worked something serious for those four hours, and I was madd tired. Dad came to pick me up, and as soon as I got in the car my phone was ringing. Chase! Finally!

"Yo bro! you good?!?!"

"Yo man I'm good. It's crazy though."

"You talk to your mom?"

"Yeah, I just got off wit' her."

"Yo bro, you gotta turn yourself in."

"You crazy! They already sayin' I snitch cuz they got Twiz and I don't even know this dude. I don't know neither one of those dudes. All I know is Twiz and Cuddy or Buddy; whatever his name is, but for real I don't even know those cats."

"Well then maybe you do need to lay low. I don't know bro."

"Yo I gotta go. I'll hit you back later."

"Aight bro. Be safe."

"Yeah bro."

"Peace."

"Peace."

As soon as I hung up the phone, Dad looks over at me.

"Was that Chase?"

"Yes sir."

"Was Chase a part of the robbery?"

"I think so."

Dad was real quiet. He always gets like that when he's really mad or when he's thinking really hard. This time I can't tell which one he's on right now. Maybe he's both. I know he knows Dre's dad. Him, Aunt Sheila, Dad, they all grew up together. Dre and Chase are actually nicknames. Dre is short for Andre. And Chase got his name because Aunt Sheila said when he was a baby he was so fast she had to chase him around so she started calling him "My Little Chase," and it just stuck. But Chase's real name is Andre. They both got their name from their uncle who drowned when they were young. Dad said he remembers going to that funeral, and how it was so sad because he was such a good kid and everybody liked him.

So Dad didn't even say a word. He just drove straight to Dre's dad's house. As soon as he walked in the door Dre's dad just grabbed him and he was crying but smiling all at the same time.

"Man it's good to see you brotha."

"Man, I'm sorry it's on these terms."

"Hey man, I was just talkin' to him the other day and tellin' him he needs to slow down and now look what he done…"

He just broke down right there. Dad just grabbed him and they're just standing there. Dre's dad's just standin' there cryin' and Dad's just holdin' him. Everybody was just lookin' at them. There was a lot of people there. Miss Kasey was there and her brother Terrence. Dre's grandma was there, and there was a whole bunch of other people I've never seen before. Then he started wiping his eyes and taking long breaths like he was trying hard not to cry. Then he turned and looked at me.

"What's up young brotha? You still beatin' up on 'em on that court?"

"Tryin'."

"I hear you brotha. I hear you. Hey look, y'all c'mon in here and get something to eat. We got too much food in here. People been bringin' it by all day."

Dad just got something to drink and then they sat down and started talkin' again. But I was hungry 'cause I hadn't really eaten all day so I got a big plate. The TV was on ESPN, but all they were talkin' about was baseball and I couldn't just sit in there with all those people. It was too sad in there, so I went outside.

That's when I remembered that I never did call Jade back. I really didn't want to talk to her, but I didn't have nothing else to do. She came out the gate like she's super worried.

"Hey."

"Sup?"

"Is Chase your cousin?"

"We not blood, but he's like my brother, I known him all my life. Why?"

"Cuz they talkin' bout him sayin' he snitch, and I don't really know him like that so I don't really know that he snitch, but I think people sayin' it cause Kudi said it. Now he got everybody in the PJs thinkin' it and spreadin' it. Kudi is sheisty though. He be takin' advantage of these young boys around here. I wouldn't trust him at all. I hope Chase is ok though."

"Yeah. He'll be alright. Wussup witchu though?"

"I'm good. I'm 'bout to go outta town, and see my cousins in Texas."

"Texas? Where at in Texas?"

"Houston."

"How your people get way out in Texas?!"

"My aunt and uncle are in the military. They been livin' out there for a long time. My aunt always buys me a ticket and lets me come visit. That's how I started likin' horses and stuff 'cause when we was little she used to take me and my cousins to rodeos and stuff all the time."

"So what, you wanna be a cowgirl when you grow up?"

"I don't know…maybe. I'm still thinkin' 'bout it."

"Girl please."

We both laughin'. We talked for a while, but then Dad was ready to go. So I told her I'd call her back. I don't know man she's madd cool, but I just can't get over the fact that the whole hood done ran through her like that. She's one of the coolest chicks I ever met though. I already know she's feelin' me, but if she try and call me when she's in Texas then I really know wussup.

When we got in the car Dad told me that Dre's Dad was talking about pressing charges because Dre was shot multiple times in the back and they didn't find a weapon on him. So it seems like he was trying to run away and not shootin' at the cops like they were tryin' to make it seem on the news.

"Jason said that they are looking for Chase and one other guy."

"I don't know him, but people say his name is Kudi."

"It's a shame that we lost one more young black man to violence in the streets."

Well that was Tuesday. Wednesday, Chase called me and said he had just left the police station. He said they let him go and that he wasn't a suspect, they just wanted to question him because they had heard he was close to Dre and wanted to know about Dre's associates. Thursday, word must've got out that Chase talked to the Police because now it's really goin' around that Chase is a snitch. Mitch sent me a text and said that they put his name on the snitch list. Friday, I call Chase to see what's goin' on and he tells me that this dude Kudi got his number from somebody and called him, but he told him about what happened with the police just to let him know he's not no snitch and everything's cool. So Saturday everybody was talkin' 'bout goin' to that concert. I don't even really like concerts so I'm not tryin' to go at all.

Mitch called me last minute askin' me if I wanted to go 'cause somebody at the radio station gave him a hook-up.

"Naw, I'm cool. I don't like J-Millz or Lil Mama anyway."

"Bro!!! It's free! I got you!"

"I'm good bro. Just tell me what happens."

"Aight bro. Holla."

"Peace."

I just laid down on the couch and chilled. Fell asleep watchin' this old movie. Man, like four hours later my cousin Sharonda called me screamin' and cryin'.

"They shot Chase! They shot Chase!"

"Girl stop playin' on the phone."

"I'm not playin'...They really shot him."

"You at the concert?"

"No...the hospital!"

There's a lot of noise in the background like she was outside and the wind was blowin' or somethin'. She wasn't even really talkin' to me she was cryin' and screamin' so hard.

"Please don't let him die! Please don't let him die!!! Pleeeease!"

"Sharonda! Sharonda!"

She wasn't even answering but then Clint took the phone.

"Hello?"

"Who is this?"

"This is Clint. Who is this?"

"Clint! This A.J. What happened?"

"A.J., man, we're standin' outside after the concert let out; just kinda posted up. It's crowded so you couldn't really see. But then all I saw was this dude came walked right up to us. Walked right up to Chase. He was like 'Stop Snitchin.' He shot him like three times, then he ran. I couldn't see his face 'cause he had on a hoody and he had a bandana around his face. It happened so fast."

"No!...No!...No!...No!...No!...Where y'all at?!"

"St. Joseph's."

"I'm comin' right now!"

I had tears comin' down so Dad was just lookin' at me. He knew it was serious.

"Chase got shot. Can you take me to the hospital?"

By the time we got there he was already dead. Everybody was in the ER just cryin'. Clint and Sharonda was standin' outside by the door, and everybody else was in the waiting room. Mitch had blood all over his clothes. He was just sittin' there quiet. I didn't know what to say or do. It was like the room was spinning. I couldn't help but think about when my mom died and we were all in this same emergency room. Then Aunt Sheila came in the door. She was screamin' off top.

"Where my baby?!?! Where my baby?!?!"

She tried to go straight back through the double doors, but the security guard and the doctors grabbed her up. She was still screamin'.

"I wanna see my baby! I wanna see my baby!"

"We can't let you go back yet ma'am."

Then she just melted and she was on the floor cryin'. Somebody picked her up and she was totally limp like she was a rag doll. She was just cryin' the whole time. Everybody else was just sitting there. Speechless.

Finally they came out and said that we could go back and see him, but only two at a time. And only the family could come. Aunt Sheila looked around and called me to go back with her. I'll never forget the feeling I got when we went back.

The nurse led us in the back to the room where Chase's body was. There were white curtains everywhere. It seemed like a maze of curtains. Then she pulled back this one curtain and there were two chairs there. And there was Chase. I remember feeling like I had a giant hole in my chest. I felt frozen like I couldn't move. Aunt Sheila just fell on him. She was just screamin'.

"Why? Why? My baby! My baby!"

I was just standing there frozen. I don't even remember what else happened that night. All I remember is up to the point when I saw Chase layin' on that table. That's all I remember. I will never forget that sight. I will never forget that feeling.

The next day, I stayed in bed super late. I woke up madd late, but even after I woke up I just laid in the bed. I remember layin' there thinkin'; "Normally I would be playin' ball today, but man...Chase... I can't play with no other PG. So I just laid there. I guess I was still kinda numb. I couldn't believe he was really gone and that he was never comin' back. I couldn't really wrap my mind around it, but I knew it was real. It felt real...too real.

I finally dragged myself outta bed around one. Everybody was textin' me sayin' that they were goin' to Aunt Sheila's house and they wanted me to come through. Dad was down, so we rolled to Aunt Sheila's house. When we got there, the whole crew was already there. Everybody was pretty much hanging around outside. There was a whole bunch of people over there. I guess people already knew about Dre and they know that the two of them were related, so everybody is feeling extra sorry for the family.

We're all sitting outside and then Mitch said, "Somebody told me it was Meech that shot him."

"Meech from Northview?"

"Yeah."

"Do he even ride wit' Kudi like that?"

"I don't know, but cats'll do anything to get paid these days."

I was just sittin' there in a daze. I heard the conversation, but I was just still trying to piece together the timeline of the week.

"Man I don't know Meech and I don't wanna know him. All I wanna know is what happened?

"Bro, it happened so fast. He just walked right up..."

"Naw, naw. I'm sayin' how did Chase even get caught up in this craziness?"

"Well this is what I heard. Kudi, Twiz, and Dre was already planning to rob the spot, but they wanted a lookout. Kudi said to 'get one of the young dudes from around the way,' but Dre was like 'naw, I already got somebody in mind.' And I guess that's when he went and got Chase. So Chase was supposed to be the lookout, Dre was the driver, Twiz had the gun on the owner, and Kudi was on the register. It just so happened when they was comin' out the cops was drivin' by. Chase must've seen them and dipped out real quick. I guess they never even noticed him. Twiz came runnin' out and a cop was like, 'freeze.' Twiz starts bustin' at the cops and hit one of them and the cops are bustin' back. I guess Dre got out the car and tried to run in the opposite direction and he got bullets in the back. Kudi probably saw the cops, heard the gunshots and ran out the back door. So the cop stops to help his partner and everybody got away. Meanwhile, nobody really knows Chase, he dipped first. They heard the cops came to his house, and nobody knew where he was. So now it makes it easier for everybody to believe that he snitched."

"Well, I know he didn't snitch. He told me the cops told him that he wasn't even a suspect."

"I guess they weren't tryin' to hear that."

Then everybody was just quiet again. Everybody was just thinking I guess.

The next day they had Dre's funeral. I couldn't even go to that. Too much. Too sad. Dad went. I just stayed home. I knew I couldn't do two funerals in one week. Even if they were spread apart.

The week went by super slow. But Friday finally came. The funeral was crazy. Aunt Sheila asked me to walk in with the family. When we walked in, she was first in line right behind the pastors. When she got to the coffin, she broke down again. She was holdin' on to the coffin and she just had her head on his chest. She stood there for a long time, but then Dre's dad pulled her away and sat down with her. When I looked at him, I was numb again. I was staring at him and I could of sworn that I saw him breathin'. I guess I still couldn't really believe that he was gone. I sat down in the row right behind Aunt Sheila. When they started to close the casket, I think that's when it hit me.

It's like somebody turned the water on inside my eyes. I was quiet but I couldn't stop the tears from coming down. My nose was running and everything. But then a lady at the end of the row passed me some tissue. "Thanks." I wasn't even paying attention to what everybody was saying. I was sitting there thinkin', "He's never comin' back. He's never comin' back. No more freestyles. No more off the backboard alleys. No more girls. No more jokes. No more nothing. He's really never comin' back." After a while I felt really tired, but then the pastor started preachin'. I always listen to Pastor Howard preach cause he's kinda young like in his 30s and he be usin' slang and stuff in his sermons. It's always stuff young people can relate to. So when he started talkin', I sat up and tried to listen.

He started it off talkin' about this conversation that he had wit' Aunt Sheila right after Chase got shot. He said she told him to, "Keep it real like you always do. Tell those young people what's waitin' for them out there in them streets." Then he said, "My mother always taught me to respect my elders and do what I'm told. So, Imma do exactly what Sister Freeman asked me to do." He only read one verse. The crazy thing was it was from the very same chapter that I read on the night that Dre got shot. Somethin' about wisdom standin' out on the street corner and yelling at us. He talked about how our parents are yelling at us. Our teachers are yelling at us. The preachers are yelling at us. Chase and Dre's blood is yelling at us. But violence, crime, drugs, and sex is yelling at us too. So, when are we gonna start listening? And who are we gonna listen to? It was deep.

After the burial, we went back to the church to eat. That's when Aunt Sheila pulled me to the side. I'll never forget what she said.

"You lost your mom, and now I lost my son. Well now, I'm adopting you. And I'm not gonna lose you too."

"Yes ma'am."

"You listen to your Father. He's a wise man, and he knows what's best for you. Okay?"

"Yes ma'am."

"And you make sure you come and see me. Don't stop comin' over because Chase ain't here no more."

"Yes ma'am."

"And stop sayin' 'yes ma'am.' You make me feel so old."

She was wiping her eyes because she was starting to cry. Crazy thing; I was about to cry too. I miss Chase so much already.

"Yes ma'a...I mean...okay."

"I love you baby."

"I love you too."

"Now come on. Let's go in here and get somethin' to eat."

About a week later I decided to go by Chase's grave and see if his headstone was up yet. It wasn't, so I went by Aunt Sheila's to say hi. She told me they told her that it would be at least another week before they could get it up. We looked at some of the old newspaper clippings with me and Chase in them, and we talked a little bit. She asked me if I was ready to go back to school, stuff like that. I couldn't stay long.

I miss my bro Chase.

6

NO THANKS

"...put a knife to your throat if you are given to gluttony"

I asked Uncle Brian for a few days off so I could go to this scouting camp and he said "No problem." Then he was talkin' about how I've done such a good job the past couple of months. I have to admit that it's been kinda cool workin' here with him, but I don't think I could do this kinda work for a living. That's another reason why I'm not tryin' to miss this camp.

It's called The Swish Hoops Exposure Camp. My coach gave a few of us the flyer a few months back and told us we should try to go. He said he couldn't get any money to help us, but he did say he would drive us up there. Chase was supposed to go too but...yeah, you know how that story ends. So when the time came to go to the camp me and Mitch were talkin', and we were both sayin' how we gotta do it big at the camp for Chase. We both bought black sleeves to wear every game for Chase. He used to wear one of those sleeves every game. Dude thought he was an NBA all-star with that sleeve on.

So we got to the hotel kinda early, then they checked us in at the registration table in the lobby. We went to our rooms and chilled for a little bit, and then they loaded us up in vans and took us to the gym. The gym was huge! There was two full college size courts side by side. And there was a big space in between with round tables and chairs with bleachers all around. When we came in they told us our team assignments. They gave everybody reversible black and white jerseys, but they all had different numbers. I was number 127.

It was kinda weird at first. I mean, you never see real game jerseys with those high numbers on them. But I found out that this is the system they use to identify the players. The scouts have a sheet with everybody's name and number on it. They make sure everybody has a different number so that when the scouts are looking at you, they know exactly who you are. It's like a basketball auction.

We were looking at the rosters and we couldn't believe it. Everybody was tall. I remember thinkin', "Some of these dudes must be lyin'." All I saw was 6'6", 6'4", 6'8", 6'6", 6'6", 6'2", 6'10", 6'8". There was only a handful of guys there below 6 feet. I'll never forget this one cat though. He was 5'7", but he had the most springs out of the whole camp. Every time he took off it looked like his head was gonna hit the rim. Homie could jump. He wasn't that good though.

My team didn't play till later so I just chilled and watched Mitch's game. It was a dunk-fest. In like the first play of the game some dude caught a fast break and dunked backwards on this dude. Then, this one dude came through the lane and dunked on like three people. And, Mitch got dunked on by this 6'10" dude. They were ballin'.

I was a little worried after watchin' Mitch's game, but in my first game I did it big too. I was hype during warm-up but I didn't say much. I just kept it cool. I knew I was gonna have a good game. I could feel it. When the game started I missed my first "J", but I heated up real quick. I hit two threes in a row and got two steals for easy dunks. Ten points early in the first half. Then the best part of the game for me. One of my teammates got a steal and pushed the ball to half court. Somebody reached in on him so he threw it to me. The thing was, he kinda threw it past me to my left hand side. There was a guy rushing towards the ball so I dribbled it behind my back real quick. It was happening really fast and I was right in front of the goal. But there was another guy to my right so the only thing I had time and space to do was grab it, jump, spin off him, and lay it up. Before I realized all that happened I saw the ball dropping through the net and when I go get back on defense I saw the other team's bench hiding their faces. Everybody was like, "Oooooooohhhh!" A 360° layup! I hadn't thought about it, or planned it, or even tried it before. It just happened. I finished the game with twenty-four points. The problem was none of the scouts even saw it.

The scouts weren't even there yet and so it's almost like the game never happened. But it felt good though. It felt real good. There were some real ballers there and it let me know that I could play with the best of them. Later my camp coach told me that my offensive game looked good, but he wanted to see more defense out of me. So the next game I focused more on defense and grabbing rebounds. That game, I had 15 points, 10 rebounds, and 4 steals. Good game I thought. Not as good offensively as the first game. There were more scouts there for this one, but only one asked to speak with me—a small division-1 school, Valley State University. It went well too. He said they were looking for somebody like me and that I might need to work on my ball handling in case I had to switch to point because of my size, but that they could use a scoring point guard. There were a few major division-1 schools, small division-1s and even some D-2 schools there. It was a wide variety. At the end of the camp I was a little disappointed that more scouts didn't talk to me, but I was cool because I knew I played well. When I got home I told Dad that "I did my best." Then he said, "That's all I ask."

Then school started. I was so tired of working every day, all day, that all of a sudden school didn't seem hard at all. I was so ready to get back. I was thinking hard from the very beginning and trying to hype myself up like, "I wanna try and work hard this year. I'm gonna do my best and make good grades this year." On the first day of school we got a new book to read in English class. She got us readin' this book about the Holocaust. I don't really wanna read this but after all that Bible readin' I did this summer I might as well keep it goin'. So I already know, senior level English is a beast, but I'm gonna get it in this year.

Then, in the second week of school, Coach Hendricks called me into the office and said that he got a call from the coach at Valley State and that they wanted me to come up for a visit.

"Are you serious?!?!?!"

"Yeah, son. They said that they're really interested in you."

"So what do I do next? When do they want me to come."

"Well you need to call them and schedule it, but he said they'd like you to come within the next few weeks."

"Wow coach!!! Thanks! Thanks a lot!!!"

"Don't thank me, thank yourself. He said he was really impressed with your play at exposure camp."

"Wow!"

"So look son, here's the phone number. Make that phone call. And then let me know how it goes."

"Will do coach. Thanks again!"

"No problem. And hey...Congratulations!"

"Thanks coach."

I was so amped! It's one of the greatest feelings in the world to have a college pursuing you. It kinda says, "you're legit." I made the phone call as soon as I left coach's office. He said they were looking forward to having me and that the week after next would be best. So, second week of September. Right as I was getting off the phone Mitch was walking toward me.

"Nice!"

"What happened?"

"Bro, I got a campus visit at State!"

"Word?!?!"

"Word."

"Yo, didn't you talk to them at exposure camp?"

"Yeah man, they say they're really interested in me."

"So when you going?"

"Two weeks from now."

"Bro, let me go with you. I'll drive you up there."

"Yo, let me talk to my dad first. He might want to go."

We had preseason workouts that day so we stayed after school and ran the bleachers, ran the track and lifted weights. I don't

BY CHRISTOPHER C. THOMPSON

think I ever worked so hard in my life. I just kept thinking about how I needed to be ready to play at the next level, and now even just a preseason workout meant so much more. When I got home and talked to Dad about the campus visit he said that he was very proud of me, but that he had a conference out of town on those same dates. So I called Mitch back and told him I was gonna need that ride after all.

"Das wassup bro! It's gon' be hot!"

"Yeah bro, I'm kinda amped."

"Yo bro, you bout to be a D-1 hooper...That's crazy!"

"Yeah man, I know...look bro, I gotta go. I'll holla at you tomorrow."

"Aight bro. Peace."

"Peace."

Those few weeks went by so slow. But it didn't matter though. I was in the weight room like never before. I was on the track, hittin' the bleachers, and in the gym like serious. I had a seriousness to my game now that was off the meter. I knew I needed to be ready.

I asked Coach Hendricks if I would be able to get an excused absence for missing school, but he said it wouldn't be a problem because it was school related. So it's kinda like a field trip I guess. When the day of my visit came I prayed and asked God for help. So I opened the Bible to read a little bit from Proverbs. When I opened the Bible it was right at Proverbs so I just started reading the first thing I saw.

When you sit to dine with a ruler,
note well what is before you,

and put a knife to your throat
if you are given to gluttony.
Do not crave his delicacies,
for that food is deceptive.
Do not wear yourself out to get rich;
do not trust your own cleverness.
Cast but a glance at riches, and they are gone,
for they will surely sprout wings
and fly off to the sky like an eagle.

I couldn't read any more. I wasn't really ready for that, but it had me thinkin'...again. It's crazy 'cause now when I read the Bible it's like God is readin' my mind. It's always talking about somethin' that I'm going through or somethin' that I'm thinkin' 'bout. When Mitch came and picked me up he was all amped up and I was still thinkin' hard about what I had just read.

"You good bro?"

"Yeah man, I'm good. Jus' thinkin'."

"Bro, you ain't got to worry. You already in there! They wouldn't wanna even talk to you and they sure wouldn't want you to come and visit if they didn't want you."

"I hear you bro."

I figured that Mitch wasn't really gonna hear me out so I didn't even say anything about what I had read. I just let it ride. The school is only a couple of hours away so the ride wasn't that long, but I was quiet for most of the way. I was just thinkin' about everything. Mitch didn't say much either. I guess he saw me chillin' out, so he just let me chill. I think the quiet was gettin' to him though. It's like he was about to bust. He looked over at me and said, "It's gon' be hard playin' without Chase this year bro."

"Bro, I was just thinkin' about that. It's crazy right?"

"You meet that new kid that coach was talkin' 'bout startin'?"

"Naw bro...and real talk...I wasn't tryin' to meet him either."

"I feel you bro."

"I don't think I can run wit' any other point. Me and Chase been hoopin' on the same team since elementary school."

"I hear dat. But check this out. Clint said he ran wit' him out at Bloomfield. He said, 'Dude is a beast'...but then, Clint says that everybody is a beast! Clint says my little sister is a beast!!"

"You don't even have a little sister."

"Exactly!"

Mitch busted out laughin'. Then, for the rest of the trip we just laughed and joked about all the funny stories we had from playin' ball. I was still gettin' at him about when that dude dunked on him at exposure camp. He tried to act like he didn't jump, but he did. We just laughed about it though.

When we got to the campus one of the assistant coaches came out and shook our hands. He gave us a tour of the gym, practice gym, weight room, locker room, and trainer's room, then he took me to the head coach's office and I met the coach and talked to him a little bit. He told me about their program, his system and some of the things that they were expecting of me. Right as we were done J.J. Strawbridge walked in and after we shook hands, coach gave him some money and told him to show us around the campus and then take us to get something to eat.

J.J. Strawbridge is a defensive coach's worst nightmare. He's cat quick, he can jump, and he can shoot the lights out. One game last year I saw one team triple-team him for the entire game. That was the first time I have ever seen somebody triple-teamed. He only had 2 points but he still had 15 assists, and they won. This guy is a certified beast!

He took us around the campus and showed us all the student spots. He showed us the dorm where all the athletes stay. It's co-ed so it's boys and girls, and they have everybody in there: baseball, softball, track, football, volleyball, and basketball; all in the same dorm. It's a mad house in there! It's just loud and out of control. I was ready to get outta there.

He showed us the athletic study hall and the library. Then he goes into this long story about how nobody ever needs to come in here because there's a special program for us, especially during the season and when we're on the road.

"Just trust me, the work is real easy so you won't have to worry about academic probation and meeting the GPA requirements. A lot of time the teacher aides will do the work for you. If you have a paper that's due and you don't really have time, they'll just do it for you. Especially, if it's one of those girls and they like you. They get paid to do it so it's like a job for them. Plus, a lot of them are planning to be teachers and professors anyway so it's just like extra practice for them."

That's when Mitch jumped in with, "So basically all y'all have to do is focus on playing ball."

"Basically, and show up when and where you're supposed to show up, and don't get into any major trouble; like with the cops or somethin'."

"Dats wassup?"

The he took us to the student center. The student center has the cafeteria, a game room, lounge, and a whole food court. After he showed us all that, then we sat down and ate. I gotta admit the food was good.

After we ate, he took us to the mall. I just bought some Nike socks and a headband, but J.J. was like, "When you get in the program you don't have to worry about none of that stuff. It's all free." And then here goes Mitch again, "Bro! You gon' be livin' like a king out here! When you gonna sign?!"

When we left the mall, he took us back to our car and then we followed him to the hotel they had us stayin' in. Aside from the trip to the mall, it wasn't a very long tour, but the coach wanted me to sit in on one of the practices in the morning, so we just gonna chill the rest of the day, spend the night, go to practice in the morning, and then we're free to go. The hotel wasn't far at all; like two or three blocks from the campus. "So I'll see you guys at practice in the morning," he said, "but first, there's a party tonight just a few blocks from here. I'll get you guys in if y'all wanna roll." I wasn't really feelin' it, but Mitch was all in from the gate.

"Yeah bro! We in there! What time?"

"I'll come scoop ya'll up at 11."

"Dats wassup!"

I didn't even say anything. I was already tired and I was really looking forward to just chillin' out at the hotel, but Mitch is all in my ear like he's tryin' to convince me to go. He's talkin' like goin' to some college party is the best thing that ever happened to him.

"Bro! Do you know how many girls is gonna be at this party?!?!"

"Lemme guess...A lot."

"Let you guess?! Let you guess?!?! This school's got some of the finest girls I've ever seen. It's like they have a special person that goes out to recruit fine girls. And you know it's gonna be poppin' at the party, 'cause you know college girls get it in. And see that's the thing, they not girls no more in college. They're women! They're independent, free, open to new things!"

And then he was standin' there starin' at me like, "You feel me?" And so, I was just standin' there starin' right back at him like, "Naw, I don't."

We went up to the room and I was so tired I just fell asleep. When I woke up it was like 10 o'clock and Mitch was already ready. I really felt like I knew what was gonna be going down and even though I wasn't really wanting in, I kinda wanted to see it for myself. On top of that, I had already been asleep for like six or seven hours and I was wide awake. Meanwhile, Mitch was super amped like we were going to the Grammy's or somethin'.

By the time we got there the place was already packed and poppin'. And I have to admit, Mitch was right. There was so many fine girls there it was like they ordered them from a catalog to keep the club stocked up like a grocery store. As soon as we walked in there was madd girls hangin on J.J. like he was already in the NBA. Homie was wildin' out. They had drinks, people was smokin' weed, and I know people were in there poppin' pills. After like five minutes Mitch was already hugged up with some girl on the dance floor. I just propped up against the wall and chilled. I was just watching, observing, takin' everything in.

After a while, Mitch came over and asked me why I wasn't dancin'.

BY CHRISTOPHER C. THOMPSON

He said that the girl he was dancin' with asked if he had any friends.

"I told her all about you bro and her and her friends wanna meet you."

"You talkin' 'bout that girl who was just using you as her personal stripper's pole? I think I'll pass."

"Bro, shorty is like supermodel status."

"Supermodels got diseases too. But, yo, seriously, I'm about to roll."

"What you mean bro, we just got here?"

"Naw bro, you're good. I'm just gonna go for a walk. I'll see you back at the room. Plus, I gotta be at practice in the mornin' anyway. Have fun bro. Just try and stay away from suspect supermodels."

"Aight bro. You sure you straight?"

"Dude are you serious? I'm straight."

"Aight bro."

I walked outside and just escaped the circus drama. I felt real tired. Not like sleepy tired. I was tired of craziness. It's the same ol' craziness at these parties. The same music, same bumpin' and grindin', same fights, same everything, same drama. I just wanted to chill. No more drama. I just walked around a little bit and I was just thinking about everything. I thought about Chase. I wish he could be here with me. I thought about my future. I thought about Dad, and Mom and everything they had ever taught me. I thought about J.J. and everything he told me. Then I got to thinking about Uncle J.J...Wow! I thought about basketball. I thought about the suspect supermodels in the club, Shayna, Keisha, Toya, Tasha, and Jade. I thought about senior year and my grades. I couldn't stop thinking about what J.J. had said about the work being easy. So then what's the point of even going to college? Why don't they just let us play ball without all the extra school stuff if it's not important?

I went back to the room, pulled out my notebook, and started writing.

I don't want any of this. I mean, I want to play basketball and all, but I don't want all the drama that comes along with being a superstar ball player. I don't want to go to school and not learn anything. I don't want people doing my school work for me. I don't want to become some self-centered superstar. I don't want to have girls drooling all over me and trying to do my work and everything else to get close to me. I don't want free nike socks and I don't want to stay in that mad house they call a dorm. I don't want to go to the NBA and spend the next ten years bouncing around to different clubs around the country, sleeping with different women, and wasting money everywhere I go.

I think about all those NBA players who end up broke, on drugs, and with baby mama drama, and I'm just not interested in all that. I remember meeting this one guy who said he was going to go to the NBA and make a difference. Now he's got baby mama drama too. His baby mama is always on the news acting crazy. Then, those guys make all that money and how many of them actually get to walk away from the game and live good? So many of those guys end up broke. They make bad investments, lose it all gambling, and some of them are just plain wasteful. I mean, why do you need a whole bunch of luxury cars anyway? I've learned enough about basketball to know where this is going. And it all starts right here. They've got groupies here in college too. I've already seen them. They were right there in that club tonight.

The verses that I read in Proverbs earlier were on point. They offer you all this stuff because they plan to use you to help the school. But I might as well put a knife to my throat and kill myself because that's

BY CHRISTOPHER C. THOMPSON

exactly what I'd be doing if I sign on and roll with all this stuff. All the mess that this stuff opens you up to could really kill you for real. Then, what you get in return is money, but money could all be gone in a hot second. All this isn't worth it. It's just not how I want to live my life. No thanks. I'm good.

Next thing I knew, I was waking up. I think I've made my mind up about coming here, but I did at least want to see what their practice was like. Practice was at 8 a.m. and Mitch was knocked out. I don't even know what time my dude got in. I didn't even try to wake him up. I just left. I was right on time. Most of the guys were already there. But it turns out that everybody who was at that party last night was late. To make it even worse, J.J. Strawbridge was the last one there. He was like 30 minutes late, and he clearly had a hangover. When he walked in, the coach was yelling like crazy. His face got all red and he was screaming about setting an example, and all kinda stuff. It was crazy. Then he told him to get in the showers and come out when he was ready to play.

After practice, I spoke with the coach. I could tell he was embarrassed about what happened. All he said was, "I hope what you took from that is that we are serious about discipline around here."

"Yes sir."

"Listen son, we're working on a real tight leash here, but we're prepared to offer you a partial scholarship. But now if you're serious, and you work hard, and prove yourself worthy, then I'll do my level best to find you some more money."

"Well coach I really appreciate the offer. I've got one more visit I want to make before I commit to anything if that's alright with you."

"That's fine son. I understand. It's wise to weigh your options first. You have my number. Gimme a call anytime."

"Thanks alot coach. I really appreciate you all inviting me up."

"My pleasure son."

"Okay coach. I'll talk to you soon."

"Alright, drive safe, and tell your dad I look forward to meeting him."

"Yes sir."

BY CHRISTOPHER C. THOMPSON

CHOOSING PATHS

"...He will direct your paths."

We got home early Tuesday afternoon. I knew Dad wouldn't be in until late tonight or tomorrow, so I called him to let him know I made it home.

"Hey Son! How'd it go?"

"It was cool. I got to sit in on one of their practices today."

"What did you think?"

"One word, Dad. Intense."

"I can imagine. Big difference from high school ball, eh?

"Big difference."

"Well listen son, I'm looking forward to hearing all about it. I'm on my way to a meeting right now. So we can talk tonight, ok?"

"Ok."

I didn't really have anything to do so I figured I'd go and shoot around a little bit. I wasn't really tryin' to play hard. I just wanted to shoot around. I couldn't stop thinkin' about the coach's offer. I hadn't changed my mind about the drama and all the extra stuff, but I couldn't just walk away from free money like that. I've always wanted to play ball on scholarship, and now here was my chance. I didn't want to just pass that up. I thought about it long and hard. As a matter of fact, I thought about it all week.

When Dad called me that night I told him about the whole thing: the campus, the gym, the weight room, locker room, the tour, the coaches, I told him I met J.J. Strawbridge, and about the athletes dorm, athletes study hall, and the study aides, and the café with the food court, the club, the girls, the practice, the hangover, the offer, everything. He was quiet for awhile and then he said, "What was your response to the offer?"

"I told him that I appreciated it, but that I still wanted to see some other schools first."

"What schools are you planning to visit?"

I don't know Dad, but I know enough to know not to accept something just because he's offering it to me."

"So maybe you do listen to what I tell you after all."

"I don't know. I do want to wait to see if anything else opens up. The thing is Dad, I'm not interested in the environment as much as I am interested in the program. And you can't just go there and lock yourself in your room everyday."

BY CHRISTOPHER C. THOMPSON

"Well son, sounds to me like you've been doing a lot of thinking."

"What would you do if you were in my shoes?"

"Well first, I would pray and ask God for guidance. Then I would ask my dad to pray that I would make the right decision."

"C'mon Dad, I'm seriously askin' for your help here."

"I'm afraid that this is something that you are going to have to wrestle with yourself. I see you thinking it through and that's good. I think you're on the right track, but whatever you choose, you have to be personally convinced and convicted that it's the best path to choose."

"You think I'll get another offer?"

"It's surely possible. But look, you haven't played your senior season yet. You have to be patient son. Let the game come to you."

"That's what Coach Hendricks always says."

"It's not just true in basketball. It goes for life as well."

"Thanks Dad."

"No problem son. Look, we'll finish this conversation later. I have a presentation in the morning that I need to prepare for. And hey, I was scheduled to come back tomorrow, but I got a few things here that I'm trying to tie down so I won't be home until Friday afternoon. Will you be alright until then?"

"Yessir. I'm straight."

"Are you sure?

"Dad...seriously? I'll be straight."

"Ok son, you be safe and I will call you later to check up on you. I love you son."

"Love you too Dad."

As soon as I got off the phone with Dad, I get this random text from Jade. "Wussup stranger?"

I was kinda shocked because really I had been givin' her the silent treatment. But at the same time she was kinda on my mind a lil' bit. So I shot her back. "Didn't yo mom ever teach you stranger danger?"

"Yea but u gotta be friendly to strangers too."

"How friendly?"

"It depends on the person."

"What if they're really friendly?"

"U still gotta get 2 no them 1st."

Now see, this is what I like about this girl. She's special. She's not simple and ghetto. She's sharp and she's got a sense of humor. So I just called her.

"Now this is very friendly!"

"What can I say? I'm a friendly person."

"Oh really now?! Seem a lot more like a stranger to me? I ain't even see you at school? You get suspended?"

"Naw man, I just got back in town a few hours ago. Me and Mitch went to this college visit."

"Where y'all go?"

"State."

"Which state? There's like five different schools wit' da word state in them?"

"Girl it's only one REAL state! Valley!"

"Last time I checked Valley lost to Morris State in the Homecoming Classic."

"That's football! We talkin' 'bout basketball. Get yo sports right. Get yo sports right."

"Ok Mr. Superstar Stranger. So you thinkin' 'bout goin' to state?!

"Yeah. They offered me a basketball scholarship."

"For real?!?!"

"Yeah."

"Wow! Well now I guess I gotta call you Mr. Scholarship Superstar Stranger."

"That name's too long."

"Ok we'll call you Triple 'S'."

"Who is we?"

"Oh I'm sorry. You haven't met us; Me, Myself, and I? You've met Me. But you might not have met myself, and I. Pleasure to make your acquaintance."

"What?!?!"

She's bustin' out laughin'. I like how she's comfortable to just be herself. She's a lil' crazy, but all these girls around here are so busy tryin' to be cute that they end up lookin' simple. I gotta admit, she messed me up with that Me, Myself and I stuff. That joint is madd corny. I'm just shakin' my head. But that's what I like about her. She's beautiful, but she's cool and crazy at the same time. If only she wasn't a closet freak she'd be perfect.

"What you mean?"

"Me, myself, and I?! Really?!"

"Yeah, we would like to congratulate you on your new scholarship. Hey lemme stop because we really wanna be friends. We don't wanna scare you away."

"Yeah. Because I'm really afraid right now."

"No. But seriously, what was it like to visit the school for something like that?"

"It was cool. You know they gonna roll out the red carpet and give you the royal treatment 'cause they want you to come to their school. They show you all the campus and the basketball facilities. Then you meet the coaches and some of the players. And everybody's talkin' to you about all the good things about coming to their school. That's interesting…"

"What?"

"I just noticed that. They talk about all the good and don't tell you any of the bad."

"That makes sense. Why would they talk about the bad?"

"Because no school is all good. Man, I want you to give it to me straight. Gimme the good and the bad and then I feel like I can choose for myself and make the best decision 'cause I got all the information. Like for instance, there was something bad that happened and the coach tried to flip it and make it seem good."

"What happened?"

"One of the players...the star player came to practice late this morning wit' a hangover. "

"How you know he had a hangover?"

"Trust me. I was there!"

"He could've had the flu or something. He could be a diabetic and had a sugar attack."

"Trust me. It was a hangover."

"How do you know?!?!"

"Cause we were at this party and he got drunk?"

"You went to a college party?"

"I told you they try to show you all this stuff to try and make you come."

"So they take you to parties?"

"Yeah. The dude I was tellin' you about, he's the best on the team. He's definitely going to the NBA after this year. They told him to show us around, so he showed us around the campus, dorms, library, all that stuff. He took us to get something to eat. He took us to the mall and after that he told us about this party they was havin' and he said he would get us in."

"So they start you on the Mr. Superstar status lifestyle real early, huh?"

"What?!?! What you mean?!"

"Nothin'...So what happened at the party?"

"What you mean nothing?!"

"Nothin'. I'm just realizing how much athletes really be wildin' out. It's cool though. Everybody gotta have their fun..."

"Wait a minute. Wait a minute. First of all, I didn't even stay at the club. I was there for like thirty minutes. Then I just went for a walk. It was crazy in there, people was pill-poppin', smokin', drinkin', girls was wildin' like crazy. Mitch had girls. J.J. had girls. They was all open, but I wasn't feelin' it."

"So you're not the superstar type after all, huh?"

"Nobody said I wasn't a superstar. I'm just not tryin' to wild out like that. And you talkin' 'bout me wildin'? What about you?!"

"What about me?!"

"I don't know. You tell me!"

"What you wanna know? What, that I don't go to clubs and don't wanna go? What you wanna know, that I'm not a virgin? Now, but that don't mean I'm the type to have sex wit' any and everybody I talk to. And it's not because church and God and all that stuff, cuz I don't even go to church. I just don't like drama, and fakeness."

"Pissshhhhh…yeah right!"

"What you mean, 'yeah right?'"

"So why they call you Jaws?"

"Oh boy, here we go with that again. A.J., I hope you got more sense than them sorry dudes you play ball wit'. First off, you need to clarify who you mean by 'they.' My mother does not call me that. My family does not call me that. And neither do my friends. I already told you I am not a virgin, but I ain't no trick either. I know exactly why they started callin' me that and I already know who you got it from. I don't like to say anything bad about the dead, but that boy Dre was real grimy. When I first moved here he was tryin' to talk to me. We talked for a lil' bit, but then he was tryin' super hard to push up on me. When I shut him down he got mad and started spreadin' these stories about all this nasty stuff I did with him and other girls and other guys. I found out later from my girls that he bet money to his ignorant friends that he could hit in less than a month. When it didn't happen, he didn't wanna be embarrassed and lose his bet so he made up all these lies. Is that what you wanna know? Well now you know. Anything else?"

Then she was just quiet. I felt so small and ignorant, and I just didn't say anything for a good minute. I knew if I said the wrong thing she was gonna bang on me. I could tell she was heated, but I believed her. She came too quick with the story and the facts. That dude Dre was kinda grimy. I knew she was waitin' on me to say something though.

"Well… I'm gonna be honest and say that what I didn't tell you was when I left the club I was thinking about you. Honestly, when I heard all that stuff I believed it at first and that's why I hadn't really hit you up. But on the real though, it never made sense to me. I really liked you from the first day we met because I thought you were so different than all these other girls around here. You are obviously physically beautiful, but I think you have the most beautiful personality I've ever seen."

"Boooy...I was two seconds from hanging up on you; so you lucky. But, thanks for the compliment. So you made your confession, now I'll make mine...I have never called a boy back like I been callin' and textin' you. It's almost like I been stalkin' you 'cause I really like you too. I knew you were different, and I like your style and your quietness. And I know you're really smart even though you hang with them silly boys."

After all that it was quiet all over again. It was like once we got everything out in the open everything was cool. It was almost like it was too serious but it was still cool though. She's madd mature so she knows how to handle herself. Then we just talked. We were on the phone for like four or five hours talking about all kinds of stuff: the future, basketball, church, God, music, TV, school, everything. We ended up falling asleep on the phone. I know we both fell asleep because I woke up at like around three o'clock wiping the drool off my face and the timer on the phone was still counting. So she was probably on the other end drooling too. So I just hung up the phone, turned off my light, and went back to sleep.

While I was getting ready for school she sent me a text.

"So u banged on me huh?"

"Lol...u sure u didn't bang on me?"

"Lol. I'm not a rude person like u. I have manners."

"What lunch u got?"

"2nd. U?"

"3rd. I'll txt u."

"K"

I didn't even see her in school, but man I couldn't stop thinkin' about her. I did see her friends in the hall. That crazy Keisha and her side-kick Tasha.

"Hiiiiiiii A.Jaaaaaayyy!"

They're all smiling and stuff so I figured they milked all the details outta Jade cause Tasha drives and they all ride to school together. I didn't really care, but I didn't really wanna give them anything extra to talk about so I just smiled and waved. I don't even remember what I said to them. Something like, "How do y'all always end up together?" But I didn't even stop; I just kept it movin'.

After school, I was gonna stay for preseason workouts. Jade must got A.J. sonar or something because before I could even text her she was walkin' up to the weight room. I think she did that on purpose 'cause she was lookin' ridiculously fine. The thing is, she doesn't even have to try hard because she's got that natural beauty. Like I've seen her in some sweats and forces and she was bangin' then. But this day, she just went in. Shorty had on this gray v-neck sweater (and when I say "v" I mean like capital "V". The sweater was long like a skirt with some black tights, high-heel black boots, and a black leather jacket. She knew what she was doin' with them clothes.

"So where you gonna be later?"

"After I leave here I'll probably go to the gym and shoot around a lil' bit."

"You mean the same one where we first met."

She looked at me with this look like "yeah I remember when we first met." I just chuckled.

"Yeah."

"Can I come?"

"What if I tell you no?"

"I'll tell you, 'you not my daddy.'"

"So then I'll say, 'Yes ma'am.' I'll text you when I leave here."

"Ok. But if I actually come out there, I hope to actually see some real basketball. Not that make believe stuff you do."

"I think you got me confused with somebody else."

"Ok. We'll see."

"We sure will."

It was like six of us there for workouts so we all went to the gym to-gether. We were all packed in Mitch's little car like clowns at the circus. When we got there, there were already some dudes there playin' 33. We all jumped in the 33 game because the high score was like 9. I'm like a 33 expert. I hardly ever lose in that game. I guess I've played it so much that I know exactly how to win. You basically make it a one-on-one game with the other guy who has the best chance of winning. If you stop him from scoring the game is basically yours.

I really need to work on my handles, but I'm always lookin' to tighten up my "J" so I shot all outside shots. I'm trying to work on shooting under pressure. Cats always play tight "D" in 33, so it's a perfect opportunity to work on shooting with somebody in your face. At first I wasn't really getting the ball, and I wasn't really trying hard to grab rebounds either, but once I got warmed up I was pretty hot. I hardly ever miss my free throws. For me it's just another opportunity to work into my rhythm.

So then Clint was like "Let's run full." People always wanna quit and play full when they're not winning. I was like, "Naw. Let's finish this first." The game was over pretty fast though. Our crew wasn't playin' for real, and the best dude out there basically quit when I started putting the tight "D" on him. We had exactly ten people, but six of them was in our crew. I knew that we would smash them, so I decided to run with the other dudes.

Chase ain't here no more, and I keep thinkin' about how that dude from State said I might have to play the point. So I'm runnin' the point to get my ball handling weight up. I wanna make our team win: coach on the floor type of thing. They were pretty wack though. The one dude had a nice shot. So I was pushin' the ball up the floor tryin' to get him an open look.

Right after the game started, guess who walks in? Who else but Jade, Keisha, and Tasha. These girls do everything together. I swear they probably go to the bathroom together. No wait…I know they go to the bathroom together. Anyway, it's always funny to watch guys at the court when pretty girls walk in. The game could be goin' strong, but dudes are gonna find a way to look and check 'em out and see who's watchin'.

Jade changed clothes. She went and put on some jeans, a hoodie, and some timbs. I gotta admit, shorty's got some serious swag. She's just so sexy, and she knows it too. But she don't be teasin' dudes. She's straight up and cool. But she bad though. Shorty real bad.

Anyway, they beat us 16 to 9. Then, nobody came; so we were like, "Run it back." They won again 12 to 8. The third game they were getting tired, so I figured I should be a little more aggressive on offense to help get my teammates open. It worked. Homie hit two threes early. Then I got a steal and an easy dunk and we were up 5-zip. They came right back and hit two threes in a row and made it 5 to 4, but then Mitch was playin' off me to keep me from penetratin' so I hit the open three. 7 to 4. We got a quick stop and made it 8-4, but then they made another run and tied it at 8. I came right down court and hit another three. Then Ryan came back and hit a three 10-up. I'm not tryin' to deuce with these guys so I try to win the game at the top of the key, but it bounced off the side of the rim. Now this little short dude hasn't done anything all day grabs the rebound and gets the quick put-back. Gotta love a garbage man. Point game. Mitch pushed it up the court and hit Ryan on the wing. I knew Ryan was gonna try and do it himself, but when he tried to make his move, he dribbled it off his leg. Out of bounds. Our ball.

"I'm ending this right now."

That's what I said to myself. I walked the ball up the court and Mitch D'd me up tight. I gave him a quick in and out crossover and went left. I took like two dribbles and everybody collapsed on me. And there's my little garbage man again right on the block. I dumped it off to him for the easy layup. Game-over 12-10.

I looked at Jade and she was just smiling. I walked over to her and I said, "Is that good enough for you?"

"You talkin' 'bout the pass or that brick you just put up a few minutes ago?"

"I'm startin' to think you're a hater."

"I'm not a hater. But I'm not a groupie either. You played alright, why didn't you go to the basket more. He would have been open every time."

I'm listenin' to this girl talk and I'm realizing that she doesn't just watch basketball, she understands it pretty well. I love that. That's sexy. Everybody left, but we stayed behind again and just talked. We were there for like an hour and then she was like, "I think you should be my boyfriend."

"And what if I say no?"

"Then I'll have you committed."

"Committed?!"

"Because clearly you're crazy if you don't think we make the perfect couple."

"And what if I say yes?"

"Then I'll kiss you."

"What if I say no?"

"Then I'll have you committed again?"

"And what if I say yes?"

"Then..."

When I kissed this girl, I could have sworn that her lips were like honey. So soft and sweet. The kiss was like BANG!!! She was so smooth.

I knew it was gonna happen. We were there kissing for a good minute. And that's when I started thinkin', "Wow! Dad's not even coming home tonight. Wow!!!" And that's when she said it...

"Ok that's enough. Stop. Stop. We 'bout to set this place on fire. Last time you walked me home. I wanna walk you home, and meet your dad."

"My dad's out of town."

At that moment I swear I wanted her to say, "Well then I'm definitely going to your house!" 'Cause at this very second, I'm all systems go.

"So can I at least walk you home?"

I don't know how I said it, 'cause it's not what I was thinkin', and it definitely wasn't what I was feelin', but I said:

"You just said we're about to set this gym on fire. What you think my house is fireproof?"

She laughed.

"What? You don't have no fire extinguisher at your house."

"We got it. I just don't know how to use it."

She busted up laughing.

"So then maybe I should meet your dad some other time."

"He's coming back tomorrow."

"Ok. Cool. Now go shower. You stink."

"Trust me, I will. A nice cold one."

She just smiled at me while she was walking away. I stood there staring at her until she was out the door and around the corner. Shorty bad. Real bad. All of my insides were rioting. There was like a mass protest going on in my body. "We want Jade! We want Jade!" But I walked home feeling real good. When I got home I took a shower...a hot one. I can't do the cold shower thing. But the shower still helped. Then I went and just laid in the bed staring at the ceiling. Wow! The very first time I've made the right decision as far as a girl is concerned. It's a good feeling.

When I got home from school the next day Dad was already home. We picked up some stuff from the store and then went out to eat. I told him about Jade and we talked some more about basketball and State. We came back home to get ready for church and after I got my clothes ready and stuff, he called me into his bedroom. When I came in the room he had the Bible open on his bed.

"I've been thinking a lot about the conversation we had today and the other day when you got home from your visit. You've been reading proverbs quite a bit lately, and I think this verse really embodies the position you're in right now. You should read it."

Trust in the LORD with all your heart
and lean not on your own understanding;
in all your ways submit to him,
and he will make your paths straight.

After I read it, I didn't really say anything. I remember readin' those verses before, but now they meant so much more. I just sat there thinkin' about where I wanted to be and what I wanted to do.

And would you believe it? We get to church in the morning and the pastor is preaching on these very same verses. He talked about how there are so many paths in life just like there are highways and interstates across the country. He said that most people don't take a map and won't ask for directions when they get lost. Or they end up asking another lost person. Then he started talkin' about how God is like GPS. He always gets us to our destination because he knows where we are and he knows all the roads. He said, "We need God to guide us if we want to end up at the right destination. But we definitely need him if we want to end up in Heaven."

For the first time, I was absolutely sure that God was talking directly to me. At the end of the sermon, he asked for people to come to the front if they want God to guide the rest of their lives. I knew it was just for me, so I went down front. They had me sign this card and I checked the box that said "I want to be baptized." Wow! I can't even believe what just happened. It's deep though because I really do want God to guide my life. I don't want to end up like Dre, and Chase, or Uncle J.J. or even J.J. Strawbridge. I want to live a good life. I want God to show me the way to live.

After church, I sat down and talked to the pastor. I told him about the decision that I had to make about State and how I didn't wanna become just another superstar basketball player.

"Well A.J., I believe the Lord has an awesome plan for your life. You just have to seek him to find out exactly what it is. And the fact that he is already steering you in a certain direction means that you're getting close. Have you ever considered Woodbridge? I know you know your Dad and I both went to Woodbridge. He was there before me, but you know they have a good basketball program. But it's also a place where you'll be able to grow in your relationship with God."

"Are they even division three?"

"I'm not sure, but I do know that they play a lot of different good schools."

BY CHRISTOPHER C. THOMPSON

"Do they offer scholarships?"

"I'm not sure of that either, but I do know the head coach well. He's a personal friend of mine. I can call him and talk to him for you."

"Oh wow! Thanks."

"No problem man. I'm sure he'd love to meet you."

"Hey pastor, do me a favor and don't tell my dad. He'll probably go crazy."

"No problem. I'll be praying for you man."

"Thanks a lot pastor."

"You're welcome."

He prayed for me, then I left. When I got in the car Dad said, "I am so proud of you son. When I saw you stand up, I couldn't help but think 'now that's definitely the right path.'"

"Thanks Dad."

I made the visit to Woodbridge without even telling Dad. I went to Coach Hendricks and my guidance counselor and they helped me get an excused absence. Mitch went with me again. It's not far at all so it only took us a few hours to get there and back. The meeting with the coach was really short. I had some of my game videos with me, and when we sat down to watch them the first thing he said was, "Who's that little guard? Our point just graduated and I could really use him." Me and Mitch just looked at each other. Then Mitch said, "He passed just recently."

"Really? Sorry to hear that."

He probably looked at five minutes worth of tape, and said, "Look son, I could use you right now if you were enrolled. But I'd love to have you next year. We're only NAIA and I can only give you a very small scholarship but we got a great group of guys and we are making a run at the title. So you're not coming here to lose."

"Well my Dad went here so I'm thinkin' seriously about it."

"Who's your Dad?"

"Anthony Morrow."

"No. I don't know him. But listen, here's my cell phone number. If you want to come, you gimme a call and I will start setting some things up right now. I appreciate you giving us a shot. I understand you could go to a number of different places."

"Yeah coach, I just wanna go to the right place."

"Well, you definitely came to the right place."

"I think so."

"Alright son, gimme a call."

"Yes sir."

LIGHT AND LIFE

"The path of the righteous is like the morning sun..."

It was all over the news and in the paper. Every year they do a write up on all the prep athletes and where they sign to play. They had it in bold letters: **"Sensational Scorer A.J. Morrow Signs with Small Woodbridge."** Dad didn't even know until he saw it in the paper. He sent me a text while I was at school.

"I'm in tears son. Why didn't you tell me?"

"You said that it was my decision."

"I'm so proud of you."

"Thx dad"

"Now we must focus on graduation."

"I got u dad"

Everybody kept coming up to me saying, "Where is Woodbridge? Where is Woodbridge?" They couldn't believe I was gonna go to some small school in the middle of nowhere. But, just like Dad said, I'm not really focusing on that right now. I'm just trying to focus on school right now, and getting ready for this season. The first quarter is almost over and I'm doing good so far. I had to double up on math and social studies classes to make sure I graduate on time. It's not that hard, but it's a lot of work. The extra classes mean no early dismissal, and no time for craziness.

I got one study hall period but nobody studies in there. If I didn't have so much homework I wouldn't be either. So I ask Mrs. Robinson could I just go to the library every day instead. She was cool with it, but she said I had to come to her class first and she would give me a pass to the library. So now I go to the library everyday and try to knock out some of that homework before practice. After school, I go to practice and then straight home to finish my homework. I'm gonna be a bookworm when I get to college. I don't ever want to be in this situation again.

The season came fast, and I was doing real good in school. I missed the honor roll by one "C" and I'm pretty sure I'm gonna get it for the second quarter. Before we played the first game in our season opener tournament we asked Coach if we could sew a black strip on our jerseys for Chase. He said it was cool, so the life skills teacher sewed them on for us.

We blew through the tournament and had to play Creekside in the championship game. They're our rival, and so we hate those dudes. It's mutual though. They hate us and we hate them. It's crazy too how this stuff spills over to the streets. If we see these dudes at the mall or something we don't even speak to them. And it's not even real beef, it's just basketball, but we hate them because they're our rivals and we've always hated them. Always have. Always will.

BY CHRISTOPHER C. THOMPSON

We shake hands at the tip, but it's only out of respect for the tradition of the game. We have no respect for these guys. And as soon as the ball goes up for the opening tip, it's on because we all know that beside the records and the rankings (and even this tournament trophy) we're playing for city bragging rights. And whoever wins this game is big boss until the next time we play. So from the very start we're goin' at it. Defense is extra tight and scrappy. Everybody's playing really physical.

The crowd is super hype. They're so loud that there are moments when you can barely hear your own coach and teammates talk, but the good players know how to block that stuff out. You get in a zone and it's like the court is in a giant sound-proof bubble. And every once in a while you throw the crowd a bone, by flexin' after a dunk, or raising your arms to get them hype. But when it's time to focus on the game, you just block them out.

We always go back and forth with these dudes. They beat us. We beat them. They beat us. We beat them. But the past few years we been really dustin' them off. We just got more talent than they got. The past three years since I been here, they probably beat us once. Maybe twice–max. And so this game was no different except they got this one kid Ronnie. He's a junior and he's got that basketball assassin swag. He's athletic and he can score. We go at it sometimes at the city courts. He's not that great of a shooter, but he's got a serious first step, and he's a slasher. He's got springs too. And like I said, he's got that killer instinct. He wants the ball in his hands when it really matters.

First play of the game, he's got the tight "D" on so all I had to do was jab step left and crossover to my right and then pull up real quick for the long two. "Ooooooohhhh!!!" It's super loud and the crowd is all into it. So, he wants to come right back down and get me back, but when he pulled up, I stripped him and hit Mitch on the fastbreak for the easy layup. We went back and forth all night.

He was determined to shut me down, but he's not on my level. I still finished the game with twenty-five points and seven boards, and we beat them by ten: 64-54. I like Ronnie 'cause he plays with heart. He had a good game too; 17 points, 8 boards. I know he's really gonna be the man next year when he's a senior. At the end of the game we dapped each other up. We both knew it was a good game. He's tough.

When the season was over I got selected to the All-Conference and All-State first teams. Coaches knew that I only had a verbal agreement with Woodbridge and so there were a few more that tried to come with offers. But naw, I had already made up my mind. By the time the season was over the third quarter was ending. I finally got the honor roll! I had missed it by one "C" the first quarter and then again the second quarter, but I finally got it. I'm definitely gonna graduate now so that's good.

Me and Jade were still goin' out and I swear shorty's hormones were ragin' like a forest fire. I'm not strong enough for this craziness 'cause I promise she gets more and more fine every time I see her. There's been a few times when we were by ourselves and the situation got real heated. I don't know how I got away but I always did.

This Christian thing is hard. On top of stayin' away from Jade I have a hard time listenin' to that gospel radio station. Some of the songs are alright, but most of it is stuff that my grandma would listen to. So sometimes I go right back to the hip-hop and R&B station because I like that music so much better. It's hard. I did hear this one song on the radio that had a nice beat so I went on the net and found the rest of their songs. They're alright.

The pastor said I need to read the Bible and pray everyday so that I will keep growing in my faith. On the real though, I have no idea what the Bible is talkin' about. I don't know where to start readin'. I guess it makes sense to just keep reading Proverbs for now. I read a few verses yesterday. One of them really grabbed my attention.

The path of the righteous is like the morning sun,
shining ever brighter till the full light of day.

I like how it talks about the sunrise. I always like to watch the sun come up. I think it means that when you're trying to do what's right it gets better and better; easier and easier. It's just like when you're practicing your jumpshot. The more you shoot, the better your shot gets. Or, the more you lift weights the stronger you get. It's like the more you do it, the better you get at it. I guess I'm getting better and better, just like it gets brighter and brighter when the sun comes up.

One thing I definitely wanna get better at is praying. When I pray I always end up thinking about something else. Or when I pray in the morning or at night I just end up falling asleep. Dad says that he writes his prayers sometimes. I think I can get with that because I been writing in that notebook all summer and it really helped me a lot. Here goes nothing.

God,
When I look back at how much I have changed just over the past few months all I can say is wow! But at the same time I know I got a long way to go. Help me to do what's right. Help me to keep it clean with Jade. Help me to finish the school year out strong. Help me to be a better student when I get to Woodbridge. Help me to stop listening to the negative music. Help me to understand the Bible more and just help me in general to do my part with what I'm supposed to do.

Thank you God for everything.

Amen.

As soon as I closed the notebook, I noticed that my acceptance letter from Woodbridge was right there on the desk. I've already read it like 100 times, but I read it again and I just sat there staring at it. I think I'm ready for the next level.

Until recently, I never took the time to really think about what I wanted to be besides a ball player, or what I wanted to study in college, but I think I want to study physical education or something. I already said I want to do something that has to do with young people. I wanna help them stay away from the street life. I'll teach them how to play basketball as a distraction from the hood. As a matter of fact, I think I wanna have my own youth center. I'll train kids to be good basketball players, and I'll train them to be good people.

OVERTIME

"Many women do noble things, but you surpass them all."

I went to a conference recently and heard a lady speaking about a theory that Proverbs 31 was written by Solomon as an ode to his mother Bathsheba. Though I have never heard or read anything like it, I pondered and savored the suggestion. I like the idea. Bathsheba was, after all, an embattled woman who had endured against all odds to produce (in Solomon) one of the wisest regents to ever walk the earth. Bathsheba was kidnapped, raped, her husband was murdered, and she lost her first newborn baby to the grip of death. Bathsheba had suffered much, yet her quiet strength was forged in the fires of that suffering. In the end she shined as a glowing example of God's preserving grace…or as the old folks say, "keepin' power."

One thing's for sure, though their stories are not the same, there are the sentiments of failure, loss, and brokenness that my own queen mother can relate to with a depth to which very few women I know can. Though she is no failure, she has suffered the pain of failed marriages. Though she is no loser, she too has suffered the loss of her firstborn son. If you ever have the privilege of meeting her you can ask her about the brokenness of suffering and grief and she will have much to tell you. Yet, she stands tall as a tower and pillar of strength for our family and many others.

She is strong. A hard worker, having had to work to provide for seven children on her own. She is compassionate; having taken in a son who was not her own by birth, and then caring for her own mother until her very last day. She is gentle; a natural nurturer and caregiver to so many children and people. An infectious smile (when she cares to give it). A prayer warrior par-excellence; just this morning she called me on the phone to wish me a happy birthday and before we parted she prayed for me, my ministry, and this book. She is the rock of our family and model of qualities of which I have been blessed to find in a wife of my own. Man, I love that woman...both of them

When my siblings and I were growing up, like most children, we found ourselves in trouble often. She had this one weird sort of punishment that was often employed, wherein the guilty party was made to sit in a chair right outside her bedroom and read the book of Proverbs "until I get tired." As I look back, I think it was a conspiracy that I was the one who spent more time in that chair than anyone else. (I still retain...It was Jessica's fault...she hit me first!!!) Now that I have become a professional pastor and attained some level of biblical scholarship, I do not necessarily recommend that any parent "punish" their children by forcing them to read the Bible...but I must admit...It appears to have worked out just fine.

As a matter of fact, this book that you hold in your hands is the very fruit of her labor, sacrifice, hardship, suffering and "punishments."

It worked Ma! It was not all for nought. It sunk in. We got it. We love you. I love you. Now we just got to act like it. I am because you are. I do because you did. I live because you loved. Thank you for everything. "Many women do noble things, but you surpass them all."

STUDY GUIDE

CHAPTER 1: THE SCENT OF A WOMAN

Do you think A.J. hides his true feelings about Shayna? Does he seem unsure? In your opinion, why does he think and feel the way he does?

_____

_____

What do you think A.J.'s Dad mean by the statement, "Once it's in your nose or in your clothes, it's nearly impossible to wipe away the scent of a woman."?

_____

_____

Think about the text that A.J.'s dad made him read. What lesson is in it for A.J.? What lesson is in it for you?

_____

_____

Journal

_____

_____

_____

_____

_____

_____

_____

_____

_____

BY CHRISTOPHER C. THOMPSON

CHAPTER 2: PAY NOW PLAY LATER

Why is A.J.'s dad so upset? Is he overreacting? Why or why not?

_____

_____

Have you ever taken a big risk to do something that you know you were going to be in big trouble for later? What was it and what was it that made you willing to take the risk?

_____

_____

A.J. read Proverbs 6:6-11. Read the text again closely. What are some lessons we can learn from the ant?

_____

_____

Journal

_____

_____

_____

_____

_____

_____

_____

_____

CHAPTER 3: RED-HOT SHOOTER

What does A.J. Think and feel about Uncle James? Explain.

_____

_____

Do you know anyone who was/is addicted to drugs and alcohol? What is your relationship to him? How would you describe him?

_____

_____

Proverbs 23:35 presents a really sad ending to a very sad situation. Why do you think the author ended the story like that? What could it mean?

_____

_____

Journal

_____

_____

_____

_____

_____

_____

_____

_____

_____

CHAPTER 4: TRICKS AND TRAPS

A.J. seems to be becoming more reflective about his relationships? Why do you think his perspective is changing?

_____

_____

A.J. says that Chase is reckless. Have you or anyone you know ever demonstrated this sort of recklessness in their relationships? Discuss the risks and consequences that are involved.

_____

_____

Read Proverbs 7 again. Identify some specific words or behaviors in this story that you have seen in real life.

_____

_____

Journal

_____

_____

_____

_____

_____

_____

_____

_____

CHAPTER 5: HIT A LICK

A.J. saw Dre at the gym just hours before he died? What lessons is A.J. learning about life and making good choices at this point?

_____

_____

Negative influences are all around us. How do you respond when someone tries to include you in something that is wrong, illegal or even dangerous? How can you avoid those things?

_____

_____

Proverbs 1:18 says, "These men lie in wait for their own blood. They ambush only themselves." Discuss the meaning of this verse.

_____

_____

Journal

_____

_____

_____

_____

_____

_____

_____

_____

CHAPTER 6: NO THANKS

How has AJ changed? How can you tell?

_____

_____

Have you ever been offered something that seemed good, but you knew it had the potential to harm you? Explain.

_____

_____

Read Proverbs 23:1-8. What does this passage teach us about riches and influential people who can offer us things?

_____

_____

Journal

_____

_____

_____

_____

_____

_____

_____

_____

_____

CHAPTER 7: CHOOSING PATHS

Discuss A.J.'s relationship with Jade. How has it changed? What are some possible risks?

_____

_____

Can you think of a personal experience where misinformation or a rumor nearly ruined a person's reputation? What are some practical ways we can avoid gossip and rumors?

_____

_____

Proverbs 3:5 says to, "Trust in the Lord with all your heart..." What are some ways you can demonstrate that your trust is in God?

_____

_____

Journal

_____

_____

_____

_____

_____

_____

_____

_____

_____

BY CHRISTOPHER C. THOMPSON

CHAPTER 8: LIGHT AND LIFE

Think about all of the changes that have taken place in A.J.'s life? How has your life changed recently? What changes still need to be made?

_____

_____

How does making good choices cause your life to get better? What specific choices can you make right now that will improve your life?

_____

_____

Proverbs 4:18 compares a godly life to a sunrise. What are some specific benefits to following God's ways?

_____

_____

Journal

_____

_____

_____

_____

_____

_____

_____

_____

TRAINING DAYS FOR TEACHERS

CURRICULUM STARTER KIT

On-the-way Activity

Training Days shows A.J.'s coming of age and discovery through the journaling process. Journaling helps students to learn to process their thoughts and feelings in a linear, systematic manner.

Journals are a useful tool for teaching the writing process. Journaling also serves as a excellent instrument for student self-assessment.

Have the students create their own *Training Days* Journal. Have students write a journal entry every time A.J. writes a journal entry. With each entry students should answer the following and/or similar questions:

1. What's happening in the story right now?
2. Identify a character or an event in the story that reminds you of a personal experience, or a person you know. Explain.
3. Identify a character or event in the story that reminds you something in a movie, TV or another book. Explain.
4. Is A.J. making a good or bad decision right now? Explain.
5. What would you do if you were in A.J.'s shoes would you do anything differently? Explain why or why not.

Training Days: THE MOVIE
The development team for *Training Days* wants to make this story into a feature film. Encourage students to imagine *Training Days* on

the big screen. Have them illustrate their favorite scenes from the book and write alternate endings and scenes that could be added to make the story better. They might also illustrate a scene that that is not in the story to show what it would look like.

COMPREHENSION QUESTIONS

Introduction/Tip-Off
1.   Where does the story begin?
2.   What is AJ's reaction when he sees his report card? Why do you think he reacts this way?
3.   Who is Janelle?
4.   What point of view does the narrator tell the story from?
5.   What does AJ say that signals to the reader that a flashback is about to occur? What is it that he is remembering?

Chapter 1 – The Scent of a Woman
6.   What is the setting of the story?
7.   What was the lie that Chase told at the basketball court?
8.   Who is Shayna?
9.   How does AJ rate his mom on a scale of one to ten?
10. What does AJ's dad warn him about that is hard to "wipe or wash away"? What do you think he means?
11. What came in the mail that AJ is worried about?

Chapter 2 – Play Now, pay later. Pay now, play later.
12. Why is AJ's dad upset?
13. What does AJ do to avoid his punishment?
14. What is the ultimatum that Mr. Morrow gives to AJ? What does he have to do everyday?
15. If you were in AJ's shoes what would be your thoughts? What would you say? What would you do?
16. Do you think AJ's punishment is too harsh? Why or why not?
17. What impresses AJ about the ant he reads about?
18. AJ seems annoyed about a party in the projects? Why?

Chapter 3 – Red-Hot Shooter to Bloodshot Red

19. Who is Uncle Brian and how is he related to AJ?
20. Why do they call AJ's uncle J-Red?
21. Describe Uncle James.
22. What favors does Uncle James ask of Mr. Morrow? Be specific.
23. What does AJ notice about his uncle's eyes?
24. Why does AJ seem afraid when they drop of Uncle James?
25. Do you know anyone like Uncle James? Describe them.

Chapter 4 – Tricks and Traps

26. Why is Uncle Brian so upset?
27. Who is Jade?
28. Do you think that AJ is beginning to change? Why or why not? Give specific examples to support your answer.
29. Who is Latoya?
30. Identify parallelisms between the actual events in the story and the passage that AJ reads.
31. There appears to be a bit of foreshadowing in the passage that AJ reads. Identify the specific quote. Then explain how it predicts future events in the story.

Chapter 5 – Hit a Lick

32. What is Chase's real name and why is it special?
33. What bad decision did Chase make? Explain the negative results of his choice and how it affects AJ?
34. AJ said he felt like he "had a giant hole in my chest." This is an example of what kind of figurative language? What does he mean by this?
35. Explain why Andre's family might be upset with the police. Who is Aunt Sheila? What does she tell AJ and why is it important?
36. Have you or someone you know ever been mistreated by the police? Explain.

Chapter 6 – No Thanks

37. Why does AJ ask for time off of work?

38. AJ felt good about his performance but he's a little concerned. Why?

39. AJ takes an important trip. Where does he go and who does he take with him? Describe what he observes.

40. AJ makes a very difficult and important decision. What is it and what makes his choice so special?

41. Explain how the whole experience with Chase has helped to shape AJ's decision?

42. How has AJ changed? Has AJ Solved the problem in the story? How do you know?

Chapter 7 – Choosing Paths

43. Why does AJ say, "I know enough to know not to accept something just because he's offering it to me."? Why is the statement so significant?

44. Why does AJ think it's important to hear the good and bad?

45. Why does AJ say he "felt so small and ignorant..."?

46. What was it that impressed AJ so deeply about the pastor's sermon?

47. Why did AJ's dad say, "now that's definitely the right path."?

48. What is the deeper meaning?

49. Has AJ and Mr. Morrow's relationship changed since the beginning of the book to this point? In what ways? Is it a positive or negative change?

50. Analyze AJ's relationship with Jade. Explain what you think might be positive or inappropriate about their relationship.

Chapter 8 – Light and Life

51. What is Woodbridge and why is everyone so surprised?

52. Who is Ronnie? What is it that AJ likes about Ronnie?

53. AJ says that he likes watching the sunrise. Why is the sun symbolic? What does it represent for AJ?

54. What does AJ say he wants to get better at?

55. Why does AJ keep writing in his journal?
56. What does AJ say he wants them to do for the youth?

Reflection/Essay Questions

57. What is the primary conflict in the story? Explain what kind of conflict is it and how it manifests in the story?
58. Describe one of the secondary conflicts in the story? Explain what kind of conflict is it and how it manifests in the story?
59. Which character in the story resembles you the most? Why?
60. Identify a character in the story that reminds you of someone you know. How are they similar? How are they different?
61. One of the major themes of the book is making good choices. Explain how the various characters made good or bad choices and how it affected them.
62. One of the themes in the book is following the wisdom of parents and mentors. How do the characters in the story manifest this theme?
63. The concept/campaign "Stop Snitchin" promotes non-co-operation with police. Based on the book, explore the challenges and limitations of this idea.
64. Describe the use of parallels in Training Days. How does this device help the reader understand the message of story?
65. Explain what you liked most about the book. Explain what you liked least.